Buzzkill

James R. Preston

Buzzkill by James R. Preston

Cover design by Heather Swaim

Rendrag Publishing 10/3/17
ISBN: 978-0-9911516-6-0 (sc)
ISBN: 978-0-9911516-7-7 (ebook)

Blank One

October 31, 1968

"Am I going to die?"

"Yes."

The teenage girl was sprawled on her back in the middle of a weed-choked field on the western edge of the Cal State Long Beach campus. Half of her face was obscured by blood, black in the moonlight. It was close to midnight, and clouds occasionally hid the moon, a waxing almost-globe. The slightly overweight man in the sharkskin suit watched curiously while her hands scrabbled in the dirt as she tried to sit up. He glanced at the clouds and wondered if there was enough light for them to see him. Then he decided probably not. Nevertheless, he looked up at the sky, searching for a speck of light moving fast. It paid to be watchful. The enemy was. He hated being afraid. He pulled his hat down lower.

He bent down and gently put his fingertips on her shoulder, pushed her back, looked down at her, and smiled. "You're going to die, but not for a long, long time. My apologies, young lady. I sometimes have a sense of humor others find difficult. You are bleeding from a scalp wound, and they–"

"Always bleed a lot. Yeah." She reached up, touched her forehead, and muttered, "It's all right, Ma. I'm only bleeding."

He pursed his lips. *How rude. She's a little smart-aleck. Like so many girls today. She's upset, of course, but I don't think she's upset enough. She doesn't look afraid. Okey-doke. We can fix that.* Then he smiled and went on. "Yes. Don't worry, my dear, help is on the way. Please don't be afraid. I mean you no harm."

The cut was on her forehead, about an inch long and an inch beneath her hairline. After glancing up to see if it was all right, she cautiously propped herself on one elbow and pushed her bangs back out of the way, revealing the jagged line of an old scar above the new cut, gleaming white in the moonlight.

Wonder how she got that? Playground accident?

Blood plastered her bouffant hairdo to the left side of her skull, where Miss Telstar had sliced her. Her plaid Bermuda shorts and pale green blouse were covered with mud. If they'd been his, he would have thrown them out, but of course, he would never roll around in the dirt, picking up goodness knew what. He pulled the handkerchief out of his coat pocket, wiped his fingers, bent, and then used it to dab at the blood dripping down her cheek. She didn't flinch, just looked at him.

I'll have to throw this handkerchief away.

One of her penny loafers was gone, lost in the chase across the field. He could see it a few feet away in the dirt. He decided not to tell her. *Limping back to the dorm with one bare foot will be good for her. Yes, it would be good. Little smart-aleck.*

She was lying on her back about ten yards from the lone tree; he thought it might be peach because one of his friends on the campus police had told him the campus had a lot of them. *Helen Borcher, flowering peach. That's it. Sometimes the breadth of my knowledge impresses even me.* The campus, on a hill on the south edge of Long Beach, was bordered by Seventh Street on the south, Atherton on the north, and Bellflower Boulevard on the west. The field was next to Bellflower.

One day, the vacant land would be filled with California Modern buildings, offices for the legions of administrators who would oversee the growing school population, but for now, it was open, mostly dirt, with that peach tree and a few struggling bushes, a perfect place for underage students at Cal State Long Beach to sit on the ground in the dark, drink beer, smoke marijuana, and talk about the British Invasion, class schedules, and the war. Always the war.

And not just reefers, they "do" more dangerous drugs, he thought darkly. *They're even proud of it, getting "buzzed." Everybody must get stoned.*

In the distance, he could hear faint sounds, laughter mostly, as the kids ran from the campus police that he had called. The kids would all escape. The campus police had little or no interest in arresting kids for beer; they just wanted to break up the party and clear the field before someone got hurt. A few escapees started chanting, "One two, three, four, what are we fighting for?" and at that, he frowned. *Your life and that of future generations, you fools. And when you are fighting for your life, there are no rules. It's win or die.* He glanced up at the sky, shivered, and looked back down at the girl. He wished there were more clouds. *And we're losing.*

He pushed the sky thoughts aside and studied the girl lying on the ground. He supposed he should regret that he'd cut her, but really, it was for her own good. She needed to know the stakes were high. And it was a small cut. Miss Telstar was very accurate. Now another chant, coming from the dorm parking lot and directed at the girls' dorm, kicked off and gained volume. This one was a spell-out: "Gimme a P!" He didn't like this either. They had no right to have a good time while the world was coming down around their ears, most of which were covered by long, dirty hair.

He was bending over her again, reaching out to blot more blood from her cheek, but thought better of it and straightened. Instead, he looked down at her, pursing his thin lips and smiling. Then, after carefully pulling up the knees of his suit pants to keep them from stretching and bagging, he crouched next to her and took off his gray snap-brim hat, revealing black hair worn long at the sides, oiled and combed back, with the top of his head covered in short hair waxed up to spikes in the front. He reached up and handed the hat to one of his men before removing a comb from his shirt pocket and running it through the sides of his hair. He carefully pulled a tissue out of a pocket pack and wiped the comb clean before sliding it back. Then he casually dropped the tissue to the ground between his shiny black wingtips. "We need names. Who is involved? Please."

"I don't know."

He stood and took his hat back. After he put it on, an ivory-handled straight razor appeared in his right hand. He flicked it open, watched her eyes widen. *Good.* "Oh, my dear, please don't be afraid. Miss Telstar won't hurt you." He took out another tissue and began wiping the blade. The sirens had stopped, the spell-out was completed to raucous laughter, and the soft scraping of the tissue on the metal was the only sound in the night. "Okey-dokey. I'll go first. I'll tell you what we know, and then you'll share. All right? Of course it is." His hand moved the tissue back and forth, caressing the shiny blade. Scrape, scrape. It always soothed him. "Miss Telstar," he murmured.

"What?"

"Oh, oh," he laughed. "I've given a name to my razor. After the satellite, you know. The first to relay TV and phone calls." *Why did her eyes widen then? I haven't said anything scary. Yet.* He sighed. *Kids today. Who knows what they'll do?*

"Young people today have no sense of purpose." She shrugged. *I'm glad I cut her a bit.* "I suppose you're a war protester."

"We need to stop."

I need to wind this up. This child has no purpose. She will have one when I give it to her.

He was right on both counts.

The blonde girl nodded, staring at the way the moonlight reflected off the shiny blade, mesmerized by the gentle way he stroked it with the tissue. He liked that, the way the girl stared at the razor. Suddenly she blinked and started to get up again. He shook his head minutely, so she lay down. He could see that she was scared. That was good. What had happened to the kids she was with? Were they the ones he wanted? *They heard us coming and ran like cockroaches when the light went on.* He liked that line. He decided he would use it when he addressed his men. *Yes. Ran like cockroaches.*

"You are Mary Jane Bailey. I am a law enforcement official. Second, you are an informant for the Long Beach Police." She blinked and opened her mouth. "Please don't deny it. We are on the same side. You are a confidential informant, infiltrating a group known as BID. BID stands for Burn It Down. The group is composed of individuals who were kicked out of other, more reasonable groups like the Students for a Democratic Society." He smiled thinly. "Although, I must say I never in my wildest imaginings thought I would ever hear myself call the SDS reasonable." He waited for her to respond to his humor, but she just stared. "Frankly, my dear, your choice for this assignment surprised me and my friends. For one thing, you are too young to be a real confidential informant. That explains the minimal paperwork, unless . . ." he paused. *Federal involvement? Possible?* "Who recruited you? Was it a man named Wingarten? Or a detective named Terry Griswald?" She started to get up again. He shook his head. *This is not going the way it should. This child is not frightened enough.*

"Who are you?"

"What's your major?"

"Undeclared. Who are you?"

"My name is Blank, Thaddeus Blank." He flipped open a leather case and showed her a badge. "You really should have asked for identification. But you'll learn. Immediately after registering for classes, you were approached by someone who asked you to be a confidential informant. You agreed. Soon after that, there was a second contact, this time by the Long Beach police, probably an officer named Terry Griswald, who explained that he would be your liaison. We are interested in the same things the Long Beach police are, and we would very much appreciate it if we got copies of the reports you send them."

"There's this wonderful invention, maybe you've heard of it? It's called carbon paper."

"Don't you take that snippy tone with me, missy."

"Were you the one who cut me?"

"Heavens, no!"

"You just happen to carry around a straight razor? I guess you never can tell when you'll need a shave."

She's starting to recover. Not good.

"At this party, here in the field, squatting in the dirt like savages, was there LSD? Acid? Were any of the kids on acid? Tripping, was anybody tripping? Everybody was stoned, right?" *She will be impressed that I speak the language.*

"There was beer. I thought campus police handled stuff like this. They drove by, and people split, but somebody grabbed me, and then I tripped and fell, and then you were here, and my head was bleeding."

"When I was your age, beer and whiskey were the strongest intoxicants available."

"I think one girl had apple wine. Boone's Farm. Did you park in the dorm lot? If you did, you'll get a ticket."

"Are you reporting by phone? Call a certain number and speak into a tape recorder?" She just stared at him. "You will call the number I give you and repeat the report."

"I don't date older men."

He extended his hand. She hesitated only an instant and then ignored it and pushed herself to her feet. He caught her hand and, instead of releasing her, took her arm and produced a felt-tip pen. He flicked his eyes over her shoulder, and one of his men dropped his cigarette and grabbed her, holding her elbows and pulling her back against him. He pressed against her, close enough for Blank to be able to smell his cigarette breath. Blank gripped her wrist and used the marker to write a number on her arm. When he was done, he didn't release her arm at once. He held it gently – the other man still held her elbows – and ran his thumb across her palm and caressed her wrist. Then he nodded, and his man let her go, except Blank held on to her arm. At last, he released her. She jerked her arm back. Blank sighed.

"You are thinking that you will not comply with my request," he said. "That would be a mistake, missy, a serious one. Well, serious for you. What would your friends in the dorm think if they knew you were a snitch?" He smiled and patted her shoulder. *She should have flinched.* "I understand this is all new and perhaps frightening for you, but believe me, it will be all right if you just do as I say. Call Detective Griswald with your reports. Then call me and repeat them." He smiled. "You have the number."

He watched her go. Stumbling across the field, she held one hand to her forehead, but the bleeding had probably stopped. She saw the missing penny loafer and picked it up, balancing easily on one foot as she slipped it on.

He was happy, and why shouldn't he be? He was a cop, well, at least in his mind, he still was. Across the street, he could see the red lights blinking on top of the two water towers that sat between the campus and the Veterans Administration hospital. That made him feel better. *The plan is on schedule.* He frowned. *At the last, she didn't look afraid, at least, not scared enough.* He was right; he'd have to do something about that. He nodded to his men, and they began to make their way across the field. He only looked up at the sky once.

Jane

A week after the party in the field where she'd gotten cut, Jane's head wound was healing. She came back to Los Cerritos Hall after class and found an envelope in her mailbox with "Jane Bailey" scrawled on it. She set her books on a table in the common room and ripped the end off. Inside the envelope: a small, square picture, probably taken with an Instamatic, of a beautiful girl with brown hair worn long, parted in the middle with bangs down over her eyebrows. She was in three-quarter profile, standing in front of a brick wall, wearing white bellbottoms and a peasant blouse under a drab green Army field jacket, frowning and saying something to someone off-camera. Written on the back of the snapshot in smeared pencil was "Maggie Molyneaux. Health Ed."

When she turned around, the girl behind the switchboard was waving at her and pointing at the house phone on the wall.

"Hey, cutie, it's Terry." When she didn't respond, he said. "Griswald, Terry Griswald. We, uh, met the other day after registration, you know . . ."

Walking down the hill with her from the library, where students had still been lined up hopefully to get the classes they needed, he had introduced himself, shown her his badge, and proceeded to take out a pack of Tareytons and a matchbook. He'd proven that he thought he was cool when he'd stuck a smoke in his mouth and, with his thumb, bent a match down and scraped it across the striker strip. It had flared into life. He'd cupped the matchbook in his palm and lit the smoke.

Jane had said, "The Astounding One-Handed Match Trick."

He'd grinned. "Stick around, honey. You ain't seen nothin' yet."

She had decided sarcasm was not Griswald's strong suit.

And now here he was again.

"Terry, dinner starts in a half-hour, and I need to do laundry. What's up?"

"I thought you might like a burger, you know, skip the dorm food for once. We could go for a gourmet dinner at Bob's Big Boy. A fine dining spot like that is, of course, booked solid, but I can get us in. C'mon, it's kind of important. Anyway, it's Friday night." When she hesitated, he lowered his voice and said, "You got the envelope, right? With the picture?"

"Yeah. I got it."

"Well, it was from me."

"No kidding!"

"Yeah, really, I mean, no, I'm not kidding, it was from me. Oh. Got me."

Her roommate Deanna had a date with an outfielder; Jane's essay for English was pretty much done.

"I'll pick you up in a half-hour, okay?"

All at once, the idea of sitting in the TV room watching a *Star Trek* rerun with a roomful of girls – others without dates – appealed to her about as much as the Thomas Hardy novel she was supposed to read by next week. The TV room would be packed with kids, and every love scene would elicit shouts of "Work out!" from the guys in the crowd.

"I drive a British racing green Triumph TR4."

"Make it an hour. Laundry."

"I could come over and help you fold, ah, the delicates."

She hung up and muttered, "Shoot me now."

An hour later, when she stood at the top of the steps, there was no dark green sports car waiting for her. She had decided against a dress – that was going too all out – and instead selected a pair of red pedal pushers with a white sleeveless blouse and a long-sleeved fuzzy white sweater that she wore draped over her shoulders, clasped at the throat with a little gold chain. The parking lot was quiet; for once, there were plenty of spaces. Date night.

She heard voices, and when she looked to her left, she saw a little sports car with its lights off rolling slowly through a pool of light into darkness. The top was down. Then Jane realized that the car was being pushed by three dark figures, one on each side and one pushing on the rear bumper. The figure next to the driver's door turned and looked at her. The brake lights flared, the car jerked to a stop, and the figure pushing the back sprawled across the trunk. Then the driver was dragged back, half out and struggling, the brake lights went out, and the car was pushed to the end of the lot, where it bumped to a stop against the curb in the far corner, a very dark corner, in fact, the end of the lot that was closest to the open field where she'd gotten cut. Her first thought was *What's he doing down there in the dark?* That was followed by *When that guy turned, why couldn't I see his face?* Then she realized that the three figures crowded around the little convertible were dragging a fourth out over the door, standing him on his feet, and pinning him against the car. Two of them held the figure's arms – of course, it had to be Terry Griswald – while the third punched him. A quick glance right and left showed the parking lot to be completely empty, and the dorm lobby was behind her, a long way away.

Jane took the steps three at a time and sprinted toward the car, yelling as loud as she could, "Hey, get away from him! Beat it!" Two of them turned and looked at her. Closer, she saw they all had long hair. They all wore identical dark sweatshirts and ski masks. She was glad she was wearing flats as she got closer, but closer still, she began to wonder what she would do when she got there, one girl against three boys, all of them bigger than her. Then she was there, and it was too late, so like a silly girl on TV, she swung her purse at the closest one, but instead of knocking him cold, he blocked it easily with his forearm and slammed his other hand into her left shoulder, spinning her around in a complete 360 before she sat down on the pavement, hard. Her teeth clicked together, and the chain holding her sweater flipped up and hit her nose. Ski mask stood over her for a moment, staring down. He looked at her and said, "Okay, good. Let's split."

And to her amazement, they did. The two guys holding Terry turned him around and dumped him headfirst into the car. He landed face down, sprawled across the seats with his feet sticking out. Then they were piling into a VW Beetle covered with peace signs that had been parked illegally next to the Triumph and clattering away, driving out of the parking lot through the entrance.

Terry put both hands on the door, pushed himself out of the cockpit, and leaned against the car, rubbing his stomach and trying to catch his breath. When he did, he muttered, "Thanks." He stepped over to her, held out his hand, and hauled Jane to her feet.

She rubbed the shoulder that Ski Mask had hit. "De nada. What was that all about? Did you recognize any of them?" *And aren't you the one who's supposed to ask questions?*

"Shit, sorry, my keys, they took 'em, and I saw the big guy throw 'em, uh, that way, I think." He pointed toward Los Alamitos. "I heard 'em hit the pavement."

"Okay." Jane started toward the spot, looking down. "Do you have a flashlight?"

"Of course." He paused. "It's locked in the trunk."

They were scanning the pavement, trying to be organized in their search, when suddenly headlights flared, and the VW Beetle was charging down the aisle at them. Terry grabbed Jane around the waist, swung her around, and threw her onto the grassy hill at the end of the lot before diving after her. The VW swerved hard to make the turn, and for a moment, it looked like it might roll, but it slid sideways, bounced off the curb, and kept going. An arm came out of the passenger window and lobbed a beer bottle that missed them before it shattered against the pavement. The little car swerved left, then right, and then the driver regained control, and it rattled out to the street.

Panting, they both sat on the grass for a minute.

Griswald said, "They came back."

Jane said, "I noticed. Did you see the plate?"

"Covered in mud."

Jane grinned. "Well, there is good news."

"Groovy."

She got up and, after carefully looking around, walked across the lot to the boys' dorm – Alamitos Hall – and picked up his car keys. "Saw 'em in the headlights when the Bug turned the corner. By the way, wouldn't that have been a good time for you to pull out your gun?" She handed him the keys.

"Even crack detectives like me can't carry guns on campus. Jane, I'm really sorry." He twirled the keys around his index finger. They slipped off the end and flew into the darkness. "Perfect," he muttered but stepped over and picked them up again. "Well, anyway . . ."

He looked so miserable, long-sleeved button-down shirt untucked, grass stuck to the knees of his slacks, that she felt sorry for him. "What, no burger?"

"Okay, Terry, what happened? What was that all about?"

They had not spoken on the drive to Bob's. With the top down, any words would have been carried away on the wind. Terry drove the Triumph like an extension of himself, smoothly downshifting before stops, braking into corners and accelerating out. She noticed that he checked the mirrors frequently. That was okay with her; she was looking for somebody following them too, in addition to picking blades of grass off the knees of her pants and flicking them over the side. Nobody tried to run them off the road. Terry parked, got out, and opened her door. They walked past the ten-foot-tall plastic statue of the grinning Big Boy holding his burger aloft without incident. In the lobby, Terry used the pay phone to call in the attack and promised to file a report as soon as he got to the station.

A few minutes later, they were sitting in a red vinyl booth. They both ordered the combo – Big Boy burger, fries, small salad that was mostly iceberg lettuce with Thousand Island dumped on top.

When it came, Terry simply stared down at his plate and then blurted out, "I pulled up, and they just came out of nowhere. One reached in and grabbed the keys while the others pushed the car off to the corner. Then they dragged me out and pinned my arms to my sides. I mean, I couldn't fight them, really. I was lucky you showed up and scared them off. Did you recognize any of them?"

Jane picked up a fry and stared at it thoughtfully before saying, "Yeah, my x-ray vision penetrated their ski masks. What did they say before I got there?"

"Not much. Shouting hippie peace freak slogans, you know, down with pigs, up the revolution, shit, sorry, pardon my French, I mean, stuff like that. I'd say they knew I was a cop."

"No shit, Sherlock." He flushed. She reached across the table and patted his hand. "Hey, it's okay." Jane wasn't exactly sure what "it" was, or if it was really okay, but it seemed to make the tall young cop feel better. He picked up a fork and poked at his lettuce.

"I was in the top half of my class in unarmed combat," he muttered. "If I'd been able to get all the way out of the car . . ." He dropped his fork, worked a finger into his collar, and slid it back and forth before giving up and jerking his tie loose. Then he blurted out, "It's not supposed to be like this! You know, it just isn't."

The waitress came by and refilled Terry's coffee cup. When she had returned to the counter, Jane said, "Absolutely. I agree. What's not supposed to be like what?"

"Take this seriously, dammit! Sorry, but this, this is not a game."

It's not?

"All right, you want serious? There's this girl, I read about it in the paper, some school back east, she's living with her boyfriend off campus, and they want to kick her out of school for it. Yeah, things are changing."

"Huh? What does that have to do–"

"Never mind. Like what?" Jane decided conversations with Terry were always going to be difficult.

"You know," he said finally, almost too soft for her to hear. "You rescuing me."

"The old stereotypes and role models are changing. Women are free. Up the revolution! Gimme a match so I can burn my bra!" She clutched a fork in her hand and waved it dramatically.

"Huh?"

"You say 'huh' a lot. I read most of that on a women's lib poster."

"Oh. You never answered."

"Make sense before I stab you with my fork. And if you say 'huh,' I'll stab you anyway."

"C'mon, Jane. Did you know those guys?"

"No."

"You're sure?"

"Okay, you got me. It was my brothers. They don't like me going out with cops."

"What? But – oh. You didn't mean it."

"Terry, who knew you were picking me up?"

"Huh? Nobody."

Jane picked up her burger and took a bite. The flagship burger from Bob's was of course called the Big Boy – two small patties, three slices of bun, lots of sauce. Add chopped raw onions and a few shakes of Bob's Secret Seasoning, and it made a great burger. "Not bad at all."

"Yeah, I like it too." He hadn't touched his yet.

Chewing, she drummed her nails on the table. "I thought cops had to always be available, tell people where they'd be." Holding up the burger as a microphone, she did a passable Broderick Crawford growl: "Ten-four, unit two-five at the donut shop."

"Whoa, you know police procedure. Is your dad a cop?"

Mistake. "Nah. He's an accountant." *Two mistakes. I need to be more careful.* "I got it from TV. My dad's retired."

Griswald shook his head. "You can be in an undisclosed location when you're meeting a confidential informant. And you're sort of–"

Jane sighed and ate some salad. "Unofficial. Okay, so you're just driving around in your jazzy sports car, and you think, 'Hey, I think I'll find a phone and call Jane.' Something like that."

"I wanted to see if you got the envelope."

"Where were you when you made the call?"

"Well, at the station, not out driving around. I needed to secure my weapon before coming on campus." His face closed, and his hand stopped with the burger halfway to his mouth. "You think a cop sent those guys? Impossible." But he didn't sound certain.

"Okay. What about the envelope and the picture? Who is this girl?"

"Did you bring it with you?" She nodded. He made a "come on" gesture with the hand not holding the burger. She pulled the little envelope out of her purse and slid it across the table to him. "Okay." He carefully looked around the room before setting down the burger, taking out the snapshot, and continuing. "Her name is Maggie Molyneaux. She's in your health ed class, and we think she's part of that group called BID, which stands for Burn It Down. Radical, *very* radical, probably communists or communist sponsored. At the very least, they're all fellow travelers. We want you to get close to her, find out what they're planning." He sighed. "But I know how you feel about this CI stuff. I won't try to convince you, and I sure won't try to force you like Captain Wingarten did. But he wanted me to talk to you. I just–"

"Wait, just wait a minute, okay?" The men in suits had taught her to do this when they'd been trying to reconstruct the night her parents had been killed. *Close your eyes, honey. Think back. Think of something you heard or felt. Did he say anything?*

No! Don't go there!

Not there. Here. Tonight.

I was at the top of the steps, looking down at the parking lot. Quiet. Then brake lights. Then one of them turning, looking. Looking at me. Then pushing the car. He looked back at me before I started down the stairs.

"I'll do it."

"–think they might be dangerous and I wish – huh? I mean, say that again."

"Fork, remember?" She waved it at him again. "I said I'll do it."

"Huh? I mean, great, wow, thanks. Jane, this just blows my mind. Uh, why? What made you change your mind?"

Would he believe me if I said I liked it? That I have nothing to lose because I'm damaged goods?

"First, I'm only promising to talk to this Molyneaux girl, see what she's into. If it's just a peace march or a sit-in, I won't help you. If it's something that seems like it will hurt people, I'll decide what to do then."

"Sure, sure. Great."

"And those guys tonight. What was that about? I'd like to know."

And I'd like to know how Thaddeus Blank, the psycho with his straight razor – "Miss Telstar" – knew about Griswald and the Long Beach police but not about the feds. They talked to me first, right after I enrolled, said Wingarten and Griswald would talk to me. What did they really want? Long Beach police to keep an eye on me?

He put the snapshot back in the envelope and slid it over to her. "The more I think about it, the more I think it was just a prank. Hippies hassling straights."

"No, Terry. It was a message. They were waiting for me."

"That's crazy. Look, Jane, I don't want you to get carried away with this CI stuff."

"They paused, didn't they? Hesitated."

"Trying to grab my keys, and I almost got his arm, and if I had, things would have been different," he said, but he sounded uncertain.

"Maybe. But one of them looked back. He looked up the steps, saw me, and that was when they started pushing the car." Terry chewed, his eyes blank.

They spent the rest of the meal talking about his job, her classes, possible majors, and, of course, the daily demonstrations across the country, marches and sit-ins to stop the war. Always the war.

Back at Cerritos Hall, they cruised slowly past the steps leading up to the glass double doors, watching for anything out of the ordinary. Nobody jumped out at them. No VW Beetles full of drug-addled peace freaks hurtled out of the darkness emitting a volley of beer bottles. The whole incident had begun to fade, as if it had been so unusual that her mind had filed it under "Unbelievable" and forgotten about it.

When he found a place to park, put the Triumph in neutral, and pulled on the emergency brake, they found themselves in something more mundane, that awkward end-of-first-date moment. Terry put his arm around her, pulling her close for a kiss. She let him have one, friendly, no passion. He pulled her closer.

"Terry, uh-uh."

For a moment, he was quiet. "Sooner or later, you will succumb to my irresistible charm."

Jane rolled her eyes. He grinned, got out, trotted around, and opened the car door for her. He walked her up the steps to the doors, where she quickly kissed him on the cheek and went inside.

Jane and Maggie Molyneaux

A week later, Jane had made only minimal progress on her undercover assignment. It had not been easy to get to know Maggie Molyneaux. In the first place, health was a general-ed requirement, so it was held in Lecture Hall 151, an auditorium that seated over a hundred, and the class was full. In the second place, Maggie was almost unapproachable. She was never late, but she always hurried in at the last minute and took a seat in the back row. She spoke to no one, just took notes and left. Monday, Jane followed her to a grassy spot on Upper Campus next to the sculpture called *Anonymous*, a pile of something like Lincoln Logs for the Jolly Green Giant. She watched while Molyneaux sat with a group of three other girls and one boy. After a few minutes, Jane turned and walked down the hill.

Wednesday, she risked being late to wait outside the doors before class until she saw the tall figure of Maggie Molyneaux, wearing her Army field jacket and a granny dress, striding up the hill from the direction of student parking.

Maggie slipped in, Jane followed, and they took seats in the back as the professor walked in. She was a spectral presence, so tall and gaunt that she looked as if her flesh had been boiled off. She wore – or rather displayed like a wire hanger – a gray wool suit over a starched white blouse with a dark blue scarf knotted around her throat.

The professor dimmed the lights, and a slide appeared on a screen behind her, a photograph of male genitalia complete with suppurating sores. She turned to stare at the slide for a moment as the class shifted uncomfortably until one of the jocks in the back stage whispered, "Mick, is that you?" One of his buddies whispered back, "You should know," and the thin woman began her lecture, droning on about venereal disease. In the row ahead of Jane, two boys opened the *Daily 49er* and started reading. Fifty minutes later, class was over.

Afterwards, Jane walked out of the lecture hall behind Maggie, caught the sleeve of her field jacket, and asked, "Hey, did you copy down the assignment? What we're supposed to read? I was just out of it and missed it." The cement patio outside of LH151 was packed with kids heading to class, carrying books, briefcases, and notebooks. The Servomation machines were doing a brisk business, dispensing Coke, tea, old-fashioned doughnuts – called lard bars by everyone – and cigarettes. Students moved alone or in small groups. There were very few shouted greetings – on a campus with thirty thousand students, it was rare to see somebody you knew by accident. A group of freaks, all wearing bellbottoms, sandals, and long hair were stared at by a cluster of four obvious fraternity pledges in matching t-shirts as a fifth pledge fed coins into a machine, pulled the handle, and retrieved a pack of Benson & Hedges. Three guys in long-sleeved plaid shirts and brown cords, and a girl in a pale green tent dress – obvious Young Republicans – were outside the doors, passing out pamphlets about the Red Menace. Another day on campus. Maggie headed down the hill toward the vast student parking lots. Jane followed.

Jane stopped walking, stumped for something to say. Then Maggie turned, flipped her hair over her shoulder, and said, "Chapter three, the first half on chancres and where they can occur and what can happen if they aren't treated." Jane noticed again that Maggie Molyneaux was beautiful, one of the most beautiful girls she'd ever seen, with a flawless complexion, glossy, long dark blonde hair that hung down to the middle of her back, and large, wide-set brown eyes so dark they seemed almost black. Under the Army jacket, she wore an ankle-length dress with a lavender paisley pattern. Jane was certain that her own outfit – sleeveless Navy blue dress that stopped two inches above her knees and cute white sweater thrown over her shoulders and held at her throat by a darling little gold chain – dropped her into a neat slot, a category labeled "Square," even though her roommate Deanna had talked her into giving up the bouffant for straight hair. The tall girl looked at Jane, looked at the YR girl handing out pamphlets, turned, and walked away.

"Thanks, thanks." Jane caught up. "I'm Jane."

There was a pause during which Jane was sure the tall girl would simply not answer, keep walking, and her career as a secret agent would be over before it really got started, but then she stopped, shifted her books to a more comfortable position on her hip, and said, "Maggie."

"Cool. Thanks, Maggie. See you Friday."

Jane turned and walked back up the hill past the double doors, not looking back. But as she turned the corner to climb the stairs to her next class, she glanced over her shoulder. Maggie had been joined by three more girls and a boy. He was shorter than the girls, with black hair parted in the middle that hung over his ears and long mutton chop sideburns that met a thick moustache. He was staring at Jane, hands shoved into the pockets of an Army field jacket, a twin to the one Maggie Molyneaux wore. Jane waved.

The three new girls weren't looking at Jane. They were staring at the boy with mutton chop sideburns.

Jane and Junior Higgins

On Friday, Jane sat next to Maggie. She had made sure to do the reading and make good notes, carefully outlining the stages of syphilis.

"Did you get it done?"

"No," Maggie whispered. "Junior had better things for me to do and I had to work."

"Who?"

All at once, Molyneaux look flustered. "Nothing."

"Oh. Well, you can use my notes if you want."

They sat through more slides. The guy in front of Maggie fell asleep and snored.

Fifty minutes later, as they were walking out, Maggie said, "Why?"

"Because she's trying to scare us away from men."

"No. What's your bag? What do you want?"

Jane stared at her. "What? Nothing. Honey, if you're that paranoid, you're really messed up. Forget it."

Jane turned away.

Maggie clutched her elbow. "Okay, okay. I'm sorry, all right? Sometimes I'm kind of–"

"Paranoid?" Kids were flowing around them, heading from one class to another, or the library, or off to a job. "Hey, you wanna get a burger?"

"No, no thanks, I–"

"My parents just sent me some money. I'm buying. C'mon. I'm sick of dorm food." The look on Maggie's face told Jane she'd guessed right – Maggie was broke and hungry.

In the cafeteria, Maggie carefully cut her burger in half, wrapped one part in a napkin, and put it in the pocket of the Army field jacket she never seemed to take off. Two girls, obvious sorority princesses, walked by and rolled their eyes at the field jacket and Maggie's leather sandals. Maggie gave them the finger. They stiffened, pursed their lips, and continued on.

"You don't seem to like sorority girls."

"Them? The sisters of I Felta Thigh? Fucking parasites." She took a small bite of her half-burger. "Does my language shock you?"

"Is it supposed to?"

"So, what's the deal?"

"What do you mean?"

"Why are you so nice? You're not a freak." All at once, the guy she'd seen before and labeled "Mutton Chop," also in a drab green Army jacket and jeans, was standing next to Maggie and looking down at Jane. While Maggie's jacket was clean, his was filthy, grimy at the cuffs and elbows, stained down the front. He sat next to Maggie, took what was left of her burger from her hand, and crammed it into his mouth. Chewing, he jerked his head at Jane and mumbled, "Who's the prom queen?"

"Junior, this is Jane."

Jane said, "Hi."

"Yeah. Ceres, I need some money."

Maggie shook her head. "No can do. Cool Your Head said they could either pay me or make rent, and they went with rent." She shrugged. "Bongs aren't selling like they used to."

"So call your fucking old man."

"Hey, man, you know I can't do that."

Junior casually slid his hand, which had been resting on Maggie's shoulder, around under her hair to the back of her neck. He looked into her eyes, smiled, and squeezed until her face contorted with pain and she pushed futilely at his arm. "Junior needs bread. You'll call the old pig and get us some, won't you, Ceres?" With his free hand, he picked up six or seven fries and shoved them in his mouth as he bobbed her head back and forth in a mockery of nodding. "That's good, honey. Junior likes that. Yes, he sure does."

Jane took a sip of her coffee, found it much too hot to drink, and set it down on the edge of the plate in front of her. It tipped over, dumping coffee across the table and into Junior's lap. His eyes widened, and he immediately let go of Maggie's neck and jumped to his feet. "Ow, shit, shit, shit, that's hot!" He was hopping around, slapping at his crotch.

"Oh, sorry, sorry. Here." Jane leaned over and poured Maggie's water down his front. For a moment, he just stood, frozen, looking down. Then he raised his eyes to Jane's. She smiled. "All better now?" A small ice cube that had adhered to his fly slipped free and slid down his leg. He actually clenched a fist and took a step around the table toward her before he realized the entire room was staring and laughing. And applauding. From the dorm side, she saw one student, the short boy who hung with her roommate Deanna and her friends – Rider, that was his name – standing, and he was not laughing. Junior didn't say a word, just swiped the sleeve of his jacket across his pants and stalked away.

Jane turned to Maggie. "Friend of yours?" The tall girl nodded, staring at Jane, open-mouthed. "Gee, he seems really nice."

Maggie found her voice. "Oh man, wow. Wow. Hey, he's not really like that. I mean, Junior's really cool, just sometimes–" Then it was like she was in a play and remembered her lines. "He loves us. He takes care of us, all of us. Our love binds us together and keeps us strong. He believes in breaking middle-class social conventions, doing things to awaken the masses and facilitate change. And he loves us." As she recited, she stared over Jane's shoulder. Once finished, she smiled and looked at Jane.

"And I'm usually such a good judge of people. Oh well." Jane looked at her watch. "I gotta go. Poli sci, and it's way up the hill by the library."

"Me too." Maggie wrapped the remaining fries in a napkin and stuffed them into the pocket with the half-burger. Then she grabbed her books, and after putting their trays on a cart pushed by a cafeteria student assistant, the two of them joined the herd heading up the hill.

"I thought you said your name was Maggie. What's with 'Ceres'?"

"Oh yeah, well, Junior gives us these family names, and, you know, they're all from space. My family name is Ceres. It's an asteroid. It's kind of nice."

What it is, is weird. "Yeah, I guess. Is it like a club or something?"

Maggie said nothing, just pulled her purse strap up higher on her shoulder.

Junior fell in step beside them as they walked. He had tied his jacket around his waist to mostly hide the large wet spot. He looked at Jane. "Uppity little piece of fluff, aren't you? Junior likes that. You stood up for your friend when you thought I was hurting her. But I did it out of love. Yes. Love. You dig? Love. Love is rare and beautiful and powerful. It binds us together and makes us strong."

He was looking at Jane intently, focused on her. She sensed that they had stopped, that people were flowing around them, that Maggie – Ceres – was watching closely, but she could not pull her eyes off Junior. She could feel the force of his personality, like heat from a furnace, and his concentration was almost a physical thing pressing on her.

"That's a great thing, that you care for Ceres like that. Please understand that everything I did I did out of love. Yes, love. Ceres was slipping, not living up to her responsibilities. We're family. Family first. We are bound by our love. I want you to understand that. It's important to me." He jerked his chin at Maggie. The tall girl promptly walked a few steps up the hill and stood patiently.

"You've been hurt," he told Jane. "I can tell. And you think you're damaged."

"No, I – What do you mean?" *How could he know? Has he read my file? One of my files? No. He couldn't have.*

"And because you think you're damaged, you're doing things you sometimes don't like. Jane, listen to Junior. It's not your fault. You just need to find people who love you. And who you can love. Our love, the love Junior shares with Ceres and Andromeda and the others, this love binds us together and keeps us strong." He took one of her hands and held it as gently as if it were an injured sparrow. "How did they die?"

She gasped and knew that he knew he was right. *He didn't read any of my files. He just looked at me and knew.*

He released her hand and smiled, pulled the jacket tighter around his waist, and strolled down the hill.

Then tall Maggie was next to her. "He's something else, isn't he?"

Jane could only nod.

Maggie said, "He's trying."

What happened? It's like waking up after a nap, muzzy-headed. Jane shook herself and said the first thing that popped into her head. "'Uppity little piece of fluff'?"

Maggie grinned. "Well, aren't you? Uppity? You reject the traditional role forced on women, and man, that's cool, really cool."

"He always treat you like that?"

"No, no, I mean..." her voice trailed off. "He cares about me, about all of us. What he does, he does out of love, to teach us and to keep us strong. And he knows us like nobody ever, ever has." They started walking up the hill.

"This is where I came in."

"So, you got a boyfriend?"

"Nope."

"Who do you hang out with?"

"Nobody in particular."

"Maybe you'd like to meet some of my friends?"

"Are they all like Mr. Gimme-Your-Lunch?"

"He did it–"

"Out of love. Yeah."

"He cares about us, really, he just–"

"Wants to break down social conventions, like the distinction between your food and his."

Maggie pursed her lips and turned to enter a women's bathroom. Jane tagged along as the tall girl stuffed her books into an empty cubicle, pulled lipstick out of her purse, and began to apply another layer of hot pink.

"Yeah, thanks, but I don't think he likes me."

Maggie capped the tube of lipstick and looked at Jane. "Oh, he does, really. Jane, he actually talked to you!"

Outside again, as they walked, Jane asked, "Are you gonna do it? Call your father?"

Maggie stared at her. "Of course. Junior's right. He's always right."

"Wow. Ok, I'll see you Monday for the next chapter in the joys of VD." They were in front of the two-story classroom building. Stairs bordered by a metal railing ran up to the walkway that connected the second-floor rooms.

Maggie smiled, said, "Love," and squeezed Jane's arm.

Jane nodded. Then she climbed the stairs to her class and sat through the lecture on Jeffersonian democracy. But her mind was on Maggie. And love. And a boy who looked at her and knew her.

Junior

Fifty minutes later, Junior watched the new girl walk down the hill after class. She didn't see him; he was good at that. A new prospect, yes, a prospect for sure. Too pretty, maybe, but Molyneaux was good looking, and that had worked out fine. His friend, the suit with the funny hair and the money, knew he was good at picking out prospects.

Junior Higgins was in the peace movement to get girls. When he'd left home and moved into the dorm at Long Beach, he'd discovered that he could talk anti-war and get laid.

He thought he should have figured it out earlier, growing up with three older sisters. It was confusing when they'd all gotten married and moved on to new lives, and he'd had a very bad senior year. But after high school graduation, that had changed. At a get-acquainted dance at Long Beach, a stoned blonde girl had started talking to him about the war. Junior hadn't had an opinion, but he'd discovered he had a gift for making guesses about her life and for saying what she wanted to hear. A week after the dance, to his amazement, he'd been fumbling with her pantyhose in the back of his van, and he'd been the happiest man on earth. A week after that, he'd told her he was broke, and she'd given him five dollars.

But if one is good, aren't two girls better? He was on his way.

He knew women – the buttons to push on the plain ones, the subtle ways of meeting their needs, creating those needs if necessary. So many girls felt lonely and needed desperately for someone to tell them they were beautiful, to love them. He knew that at a level buried so deep that asking him about it would have been like asking a fish how its gills worked.

If Junior had been a fish, he would have been a shark. Not a barracuda, they hunted in packs. No, a solitary gray shark cruising silently, mouth open, flat, expressionless eyes scanning, always questing for blood in the water, for the fish that was wounded, damaged.

And those same instincts told him this Jane was one. Damaged. Prey. And his instincts told him that some of the damaged ones wanted it, wanted to be prey.

On Monday, they were waiting for her outside LH-151, passing a Benson & Hedges menthol between them. Junior stepped up at once and stood in front of her, smiling, holding out the smoke. She shook her head. He shrugged and stuck it in his mouth. "Jane, meet the girls. Andromeda, Pleiades, and Tranquility. You know Ceres."

Andromeda wore jeans and a gray sweatshirt with cigarette burns. She was round: a round face with features squeezed into the middle, and a round head with long brown hair on slumped round shoulders that merged with minimal indication of breasts into round hips and cylindrical legs that slid into leather Birkenstock sandals with no sign of ankles. And she was big. She probably weighed as much or more than the shorter Junior.

Pleiades was even taller, taller than Andromeda, and the way she stood, leaning forward at the waist and clutching her books to her chest with her hands folded under her prominent chin, combined with her cat's eye glasses and green granny dress to make her look like a praying mantis.

The third girl wasn't really there. She was plain – not ugly, just vacant. She stared at her sandals unless Junior was speaking. Then she looked up and stared at him with her lips slightly parted. The sleeves of her faded ochre sweatshirt were pushed up, revealing old, yellowing bruises on both forearms.

Jane had found a bruise like that on her arm when she was twelve. She'd found it the next day after she'd gotten her arm loose and run into the cornfield. Away from the bad man. Into the corn. The whispering corn.

"Hi. I'm Jane–" There was an awkward moment. None of the girls spoke. Then Jane said, "Well, I gotta get to the library."

The three girls she had just met looked at Junior. Then they turned to her and said in unison, "We love you, Jane." Maggie – Ceres – said nothing, but she was smiling. One by one, they squeezed her arm, smiling.

Jane smiled weakly and started up the walkway. Junior said, "We usually hang out by the big railroad ties, you know, the sculpture. We'll walk up with you."

Again, Jane felt the force of his personality, like a strong undertow pulling an exhausted swimmer out to sea. He made you feel like you were the most important person in the world – or maybe the *only* person in the world.

In front of the double glass doors to the library, all the girls murmured again, "We love you." Junior took her right hand, lifted it to his lips, and kissed her palm. Maggie said she had a class in Fine Arts 1 and hurried off.

Jane shivered as the others moved off. One girl was on each side of Junior. Andromeda was behind him. Formation.

As she entered the library, Jane shivered again. *When he kissed my hand, I was smiling. He made me feel good.*

That night, she slept.

The First Nightmare

The breeze pushed through the corn, and the corn sighed, restless, as if the stalks were whispering to one another, telling private things in the early dark that came to the fields in the fall. It was late September, and it had been a cool year, so the harvest hadn't started yet. The corn stalks stood tall and leafy in the gathering darkness, rows that went on for miles. *He's getting close.* She ran across the cornfield, bare feet getting sliced on bits of last year's stubble. *He's getting close.* It was a dream, and in the dream, he was always getting close, and she knew it was a dream, and still she kept running. She couldn't see him despite the moonlight, but she could hear him, pounding along, swearing, using words Mommy and Daddy had told her never to say. *Closer.* With the tears streaming down her face, it was hard to see, and the corm was twice as tall as she was, but that was okay because she knew this place, played here even where they told her not to. She ran. She jumped over a shallow irrigation ditch, hoping he would not see it and fall. She ducked off the path, into the stalks, crouched and peeked out between the leaves. He cleared the distance over the ditch easily and kept coming. He was still using bad words. Then, clearly: "I'll kill you, you little bitch."

I can run and hide, and he won't find me, and when he's gone, I'll walk over to the Mortons, and they will make it all right, she thought, and in the dream, it was possible. She could hide and be safe.

But she didn't want to. Not after what he'd done.

Then the dream showed her something else. She knew she could not get away after all.

She'd let him get close when she'd hidden. Too close. She started running again, hooked left, then left again, heading back toward the house like when she played in the corn, pretending to be a princess who had escaped the castle where the evil queen had been holding her captive. In that game, she always got away.

Her parents were in the house, she knew that, but she didn't want to see them. She thought of what she'd seen.

Jump cut. No transition. *This is a dream. I need to wake up.*

He was gaining. She ran across the cornfield, bare feet getting sliced on stubble. He was gaining. Then, in the weird way of dreams, he fell again, and she was running again. *No, he hasn't fallen yet.*

Hook left. Hook left again. In the dream, she started back to the farmhouse where they lived while her father learned how to raise corn. Only, the corn was grown now, tall. The breeze pushed through the stalks, whispering, telling its secrets, indifferent to a little girl running for her life. She ran. She tripped and went down.

Jane woke up throwing her hands out to break her fall. Always the same. She never finished falling. He never caught her. She never saw what happened at the end. *I'm glad I don't have to watch the end, see his face.* Her heart was pounding, her breath ragged.

But this time, hadn't it seemed he'd been a little closer? Had he actually touched her foot, touched it with the index finger that was missing the fingernail, that was bloody, as he'd come lunging out of the corn? No, that was silly.

Yes. Closer. What about his fingernail?

Someone was pounding on the door to her room. "Bailey! Bailey, wake up! C'mon, let us in."

Bailey? Who? It took a moment for the same to sink in. *I'm Bailey.*

"Hold your horses. I'm coming, okay?" But before she went to the door, she groped under her bed and pulled out a wooden jewelry box. The key was on a cord around her neck. She opened the box and took out a business-sized envelope. She pulled out a newspaper clipping, and as she did, she thought for the thousandth time, *Stupid to keep it. Stupid.* After it had happened, the kind men in gray suits had told her to keep nothing from her old life. She carefully unfolded it and looked at the picture of the smiling family: father, mother, daughter all smiling for the camera.

The headline read: "Double murder of alleged mob witness and pregnant wife." There was no mention of a twelve-year-old girl surviving. The paper had cooperated.

The knocking started again. She carefully folded the clipping, slipped it back into the envelope, and put the box away.

"It's about time!" Deanna swept into the room, followed by Donna and Darlene. Fuzzy slippers, curlers, baby dolls, cigarette smoke, and perfume immediately made the room seem much smaller. "Bailey, we need your help." Deanna took the chair at her desk and swung her legs – so tiny that her feet didn't reach the floor. Donna perched on the edge of the desk, and Darlene plopped down next to Jane on the bed.

"Check it out, Bailey," said Darlene. "The polish is called 'Passionate Purple.'" She kicked off one of her fuzzy slippers and wiggled her toes.

Deanna said, "Darlene, no one cares."

Donna said, "Darlene, I care, deeply. Thank you for sharing this personal, intimate piece of information."

Darlene stuck out her tongue. Jane laughed. The day she'd moved in, Jane had met her roommate, Deanna, and she and the older girls, her friends known as the Three Ds, had taken Jane under their wing, showing her around campus, offering fashion advice, ("Change your hair, honey") inviting her to a candle passing for a girl who'd gotten engaged, and making her feel welcome. "Deanna, this is your room. Where's your key?"

Deanna said, "In my desk, of course. Bailey, we need your help."

From her position on Jane's desk, swinging her legs, Donna said, "We're desperate."

"Um, sure. What time is it?"

"Midnight. The witching hour."

"We're here to stir the cauldron. We had some Red Mountain." Donna was majoring in Shakespeare and baseball players, and she never let anyone forget the former. "Double, double, toil and trouble." She jumped up and went over to the mirror on the closet door and began pulling rollers the size of beer cans out of her brown hair, casually tossing them on Jane's bed. "We were going to save some for you, but–" She examined her almost roller-free hair in the mirror.

Deanna said, "But then it was gone. We were talking about the pig party."

Donna said, "Thrice and once the hedge-pig whined."

Then they were all talking at once.

"Literally."

"Pig party."

"Oink, oink."

"It'll be great! And we need another girl. You got a brush I can use?" Jane got a hairbrush for Donna.

"Woman, woman." Deanna had recently discovered *The Feminine Mystique*. "We've got a bunch of guys coming to a pig dinner on the beach, and Abby had to go home, and we need you."

"Beach party! Can you dig it?"

Jane said, "Hedge-pig? Abby went home? I'm not really awake here."

Deanna plowed on. "Right, and we wanted to invite you anyway only we couldn't find you, and it'll be a lot of fun. Please say you'll come."

"Why is it called a pig party?"

They all laughed. One of them said, "You really don't know?" Jane shook her head.

"We cook up this enormo pot of spaghetti, and there's salad and bread."

Deanna said, "And *no silverware*. Can you dig it? Total primitive-o! Everybody drinks wine and beer and eats with their hands. It's a *riot!* We did it last year, and it was *so much fun!* Dessert is chocolate cake, if you can believe it."

Donna giggled. "Last year, that leftfielder, Todd, smeared cake *all over me!*" Jane made a mental note to eat before the pig party. "And wanted to lick it off!"

"Suggested dress is a bathing suit."

"You will probably want to go into the water after we gorge ourselves on salad, spaghetti, and cake."

"Gorge."

"Oinkety oink oink. Double, double, toil and trouble."

They all chanted, "Fire burn, and cauldron bubble."

Deanna said, "We learned the words, and we're gonna do that at the party. While we cook! Total freak-out! Forget your diet, darling."

"If I say yes, will you let me go back to sleep? Never mind. When is this epic event?"

"Friday night."

"We're going down to the fire rings in Huntington. Just north of the pier."

"What can I bring?"

"Drinks. You got a fake ID, right?"

"Yeah. It's not very good." In truth, it was high-quality since it had been provided by the men in suits who had watched over her since – since what? *The cornfield. The corn. Whispering. Whispering. I was running.*

Deanna touched her shoulder. "Whoa, honey, you okay? For a minute there, you were somewhere else."

She pushed it – whatever *it* was – away. Thinking about it too much was bad. The men in suits said so. "What? I'm okay. What can I bring?" For some reason, they all looked at each other before replying. And she had not one, but three driver's licenses. One even had her correct age.

"Wine. Boone's Farm Wild Mountain goes with spaghetti. If you really want white–"

"Wrong, just *so* wrong with spaghetti." Deanna's drink of choice last year had been peppermint schnapps. Now, as a senior, she was getting sophisticated.

Donna hit her with a pillow. "Wine and your best bikini."

"Right."

Now with her hair restored, Donna started collecting the rollers. "So, who was Mr. Tall, Dark, and Drives a Sports Car?"

Deanna nudged her. "Yeah, c'mon, sweetie, tell us girls *all* about him."

Donna said, "Women."

"He's not a dormie, is he?"

"Where'd you meet him?"

"What's his name?"

"Well, c'mon, honey, say something."

Jane rolled her eyes. "His name is, Terry. I met him in front of the bookstore. He lives off-campus."

Deanna nodded at the other two D's. "All right, girls, shoo. I want a word with my roomie." At once, Donna collected the last of her rollers, and she and Darlene jumped up and left.

After the door closed, Deanna sat on the bed next to her, plucked at the hem of her pink baby doll nightie, and then looked at Jane seriously.

"Okay, honey. Woman talk. You're safe? Right?" After she said it, she got up and devoted her attention to picking up the books and lesson plans on her bed and putting them away.

Jane had a very bad moment. *Safe? I'll never be safe.* But her voice was even as she said, "Whatever do you mean, Deanna?"

The other girl rolled her eyes. "You know, The Pill? Are you on The Pill?"

And in fact, she was. She hadn't even had to lie to the doctor about "lady problems." The men in suits had cleared the way when she'd graduated from high school.

Jane smiled at Deanna and said, "Yes, I'm on the pill. It's okay. But if that's a condition of the party, I'm out. I'm not a party favor."

"No, no! Geez, what do you think we are? No, if some guy says he wants to take you home, it's up to you. Geez."

She actually slept a few hours before getting up, brushing her teeth in the community bathroom and hiking up to the cafeteria. After her usual bacon and eggs, she went to her 10 am health ed class. There was a wave of patchouli, and then Maggie slid in beside her, dressed as usual in her field jacket over a long lavender granny dress. Bending down and pretending to tie her tennis shoe, Maggie whispered, "Meeting Friday night."

"Where?"

The younger girl looked up at her suspiciously. "You'll find out when it's time, all right?"

"I've got a party to go to."

"What party?"

"Just some kids from the dorm going down to the beach."

Maggie looked at her. "You don't sound very committed to the cause. Look, Junior likes you. I mean, don't say anything to him, but he's probably going to let you join the family."

Jane shrugged. "I can't back out of the party now, and I don't even know what the cause is. Stop the war? What? What are you guys into?"

"Do you believe in what we're doing?"

Time to slip in a code word. "Pig Nation. It needs to come down."

Maggie echoed her, "Pig Nation," and she raised a fist. "So, do you believe?"

"Probably, but I'm still not sure what it is you want."

"We want to bring it down, okay? The end of the establishment."

"All right. I can dig it. I hate the war."
"Listen, we're going to do something, something big. We're not just talk, okay?"
"Like what?"
"You'll find out later."

The First Report

Transcribed from telephone report recorded by CI #47221, code name Harriet.

Name <removed at request of Supervising Agency>

Long Beach Police Department

Confidential Transcript. Duplication without Express Written Permission Is Forbidden

Contents: Transcript of Telephone Report Date <removed at request of Supervising Agency>

Confidential Informant "Harriet" 47221

Re.: Radical student group BID (tentative identification: Burn It Down) A9906-01.69

This transcript is the property of the Long Beach Police Department and is for internal use only. Permission to copy, quote from, or otherwise reveal the contents of this document is limited by law. Unauthorized use carries severe penalties.

Direct all inquiries to:

Commanding Officer

Intelligence and Covert Monitoring

Long Beach Police Department

Phone Number: <Deleted>

Transcript: Supervising Officer <Name deleted>

Case: Inquiry into Radical Student Organizations at CSULB

Case Number: <Deleted. Requestor unknown.>

<u>Description of Document</u>: Transcript of telephone recording from Confidential Informant. Prepared by <Deleted. Requestor unknown.> Date: <Deleted. Requestor unknown.> Report recorded on Toshiba reel-to-reel ¼" tape. Length Time 1 min. 9 sec.

Disposition of Toshiba tape: <Deleted. Requestor unknown.>

Transcript follows:

Uh, hi, I mean, this is my first report. My number is 47221. "Harriet." It's <inaudible>. Uh, well, I guess things are going okay. I met the subjects just like you said in health ed, and they seemed to accept me as a fellow protestor. Uh, I've met five so far, a kid called Junior and girls called Andromeda, Pleiades, and one whose name I can't remember — she's sort of a nothing — and the girl called Maggie Molyneaux. They seem to have names given to them by Junior, so I don't know the real names except for Molyneaux. So far, I haven't been to any meetings. Mostly they just sit around and smoke dope and talk about the war. What else? Maggie always wears an Army field jacket with anti-war pins on it. She must be really smart, because she's tutoring a kid from her chemistry class. I met him once outside the bookstore. That's it for now. I hope this is the kind of thing you're looking for. Okay, uh, bye.

Transcript ends.

1 of 1.

Duplication Forbidden. Duplication Forbidden. Duplication Forbidden.

Planning the Pig Party

Tuesday afternoon in the cafeteria, the Three D's waved her over to their table after lunch. Deanna rapped her coffee cup with a long, manicured nail. "Okay, the meeting is called to order. First item–" Somebody on the Greek side lobbed a dinner roll, and it arced over their table until the short kid called Rider snatched it out of the air. He muttered something and started toward the table with the roll-thrower, but two very tall guys stopped him. He still glared at the offender as they all sat down. There were a few calls of "food fight!" but it didn't take off.

Donna snorted, "The only item."

"The first item on the agenda is the Fabulous Pig Party, which is scheduled for this Friday night. Food? Donna?"

"The menu is as follows: beer, wine, beer, spaghetti, beer, bread, more wine, salad, and then cake." She grinned. "Followed by more beer and a swim."

"Sid's gang says we can use their kitchen if we cook extra for them." Deanna drank some coffee – apparently, she found it just fine, although dorm coffee was awful – and put the cup down.

In the corner of the bustling cafeteria, Jane saw a tall figure in a pin-bedecked Army coat sitting by herself, smoking, and watching Jane and the Three D's. A minute later, when the rest of the girls went off to class, Jane walked over and sat next to Maggie. The other girl spoke first.

"What are you doing with those bourgeois sorority types?"

Jane shrugged. "Deanna's my roommate. They're my friends."

"You shouldn't have friends like that."

"Oh man, I forgot to check with you about them. Geez, I'm *so sorry!* Friends like what, Maggie?"

Lowering her voice, the girl said, "Junior saw them with you yesterday, and he says those girls have no social conscience."

Jane hesitated for a moment and then said, "Maggie, I believe in the same things you do, you know that. But if it means you get to pick my friends, then I'm out." Maggie's eyes narrowed. "Unless you give me a really good reason for dumping them."

"There's a lot you don't know, but all I can say now is we've got plans, okay? Big plans. All we need is some money, and then pow! We're going to freak out a bunch of people. And no, the last thing we want you to do is dump them."

"And I might want to be part of those plans, but I have no idea what they might be. Do you see that as a problem? Because I do."

"This party is Friday night?"

"Yes."

"Where?"

"Huntington. The fire rings north of the pier."

Maggie stood. "You'll be contacted. If somebody says, 'Ferdinand,' you say, 'Dead.' Got it?"

Jane stared. "You really have a secret password? You're kidding me."

Maggie grabbed Jane's blouse and pulled her close. "We're in a war. And the establishment would like nothing better than to shut us down, okay? When you hear the word, you come to the meeting. We're your family. We love you. They don't. Nobody else does. Nobody else loves you like we do. Junior told us. Got it?"

"Let go of my blouse." The tall girl did. Jane went on. "Yeah, Maggie, I get it. I had to know if you were serious. You got it?" Jane didn't wait for an answer, just turned and walked away.

Ferdinand. Dead.

Then it came to her: last year in high school, modern history class. *Archduke Ferdinand and his wife were assassinated. It started World War I.*

Blank Two

"I'm not sure about you, not at all." Blank looked out the window of the Cadillac limo as it turned onto Bellflower Boulevard, leaving the campus. Right on Bellflower, right again on Atherton. Blank had instructed his driver to circle the campus. The confidential informant had gone to her two o'clock and then hiked back down the hill to the dorm. As she walked down State College Drive, Blank had his driver – today it was Manny – slide the black Cadillac up next to her, power the window down, and say, "Mr. Blank wants a chat. Get in."

She said, "Sure," and then waited. After a moment, Manny pulled to the curb, got out, and held the door for her to get into the back seat. Watching her closely, Blank inquired how her classes were going and then said, "I'm not sure about you." *She isn't as afraid as she should be. Obviously, she does not understand how serious this is. She doesn't understand how seriously our enemies, the ones who just launched another Soyuz, are. Another one! It's up there right now, maybe passing overhead.* He hadn't thought of that. Passing overhead, right now. He pulled out a handkerchief and wiped sudden sweat from his forehead. He was glad he hadn't gotten out of the car. *Up there now. Looking. Beeping.* He shuddered. He pulled a small spiral-bound notebook from his inside coat pocket and thumbed through it to today's date. No, it was all right. Nothing due to pass overhead for ninety-three minutes. A few days after the Sputnik launch, two professors from the University of Illinois at Urbana had used the ILLIAC computer to calculate the orbit. Now all satellites were tracked.

"Let's walk for a bit." Just to be safe, he put on his hat. He put the handkerchief back, slipped his hand into his coat pocket, and touched her smooth, ivory handle. Touching Miss Telstar always made him feel better.

The informant snapped, "Join the club. BID's not sure of me either."

"I have not received any reports."

"Nothing to say."

He was not convinced but decided to let it go. "You must gain their confidence, penetrate their inner circle."

"'Inner circle!' Look, Mr. Blank, as near as I can tell, these are just kids that smoke dope and talk about the war. So what? And you know what, I'm not sure I want to do this anymore."

"Call me Colonel Blank. Penetrate their–"

"Inner circle. Yeah, yeah. Look, I don't think they have an inner circle."

"Please do not interrupt me." *She is not cowed enough. She needs another lesson. Well, that is easily arranged.* He could still feel them, up there outside the atmosphere, circling overhead in space. *Beeping. Watching me.* He touched Miss Telstar again and noticed the informant staring at him. "Who knows what else they have?" he muttered.

"What on earth are you talking about?"

"Not earth at all." He shook his head and once again looked up. They continued to walk along Atherton, with the vacant land belonging to the school on their right and the Caddy trailing behind. "I was having dinner with my parents. Cook had just brought in dessert, it was strawberry shortcake, and Ransom, he was senior staff, Ransom came in and said something was happening. We knew it must be serious because staff never interrupted dinner. They had strict orders. My father was very strict." *That's better. She looks nervous.* "So my father had Ransom tell Cook to serve coffee in the parlor. Of course, there was no television set in the dining room, and that's where we saw it."

"The TV?"

Perhaps telling her will properly frighten her. "The first Sputnik. October 4, 1957. They were ahead of us in 1957, and they still are. Things, these things up there in space, dangerous things. Sputniks, Soyuz, and they sent a dog. A dog!" The Informant nodded, and she was edging away from him and smiling weakly. *Good. She is afraid. I can see that she understands. Perhaps she will be one of the few who really understand the danger. Perhaps it's time to put her at ease. She needs to be comfortable with me, see me as a protector – which, of course, I am. Yes, she understands. Now I'll put her at ease, relieve some of her fear.* "So, how's your home ec class? Lots of good recipes?" Now she looked confused. *What's wrong with girls today? Are they all dim-witted?*

"Uh, Friday, we're cooking spaghetti for a party."

"This party isn't out in that field, is it?" He gestured to their right.

"No, it's a beach party, down at the Huntington fire rings. There's supposed to be a red tide."

"Red Tide? Is that one of those Communist rock groups? Or some kind of dope?" She just stared at him. *This Informant is slow! How did she ever get in college?* "I made a joke."

Now she was staring at him again. "No, uh, no, it's like some kind of algae in the water."

"I know. Well, anyway, your family will certainly appreciate good, nutritious meals. What's that paper sticking out of your purse?"

It was a flyer for next week's demonstration. Maggie had stuffed it into Jane's bag. He took it from her and carefully copied down the details.

After the limo dropped the informant at Cerritos Hall, he watched her climb the steps and thought, *I was wrong. She doesn't understand.* It made him sad. Then he ran his fingers along Miss Telstar's ivory handle again and felt better. He would do what was necessary. If it made him feel bad, well, sacrifices had to be made.

Friday night – The Pig Party

The fire rings were cement circles in the sand, made to contain the fires people built to toast hot dogs and marshmallows. This late in the season, they were mostly empty.

Just before sunset, Jane declined a ride with the Three D's and took her Valiant – of course named Prince – south to Huntington, bringing a six-pack of Budweiser, a bottle of Wild Mountain, and another of Apple Wine. She parked at the south end of the public lot on Pacific Coast Highway and lugged all this stuff across the still-warm sand to the obvious party – about two dozen kids gathered around a bonfire, listening to a girl wearing a Long Beach sweatshirt, shorts, and a floppy hat while she played a guitar and sang. Jane stopped about ten yards away and watched.

Elfin little Deanna, dressed in light blue shorts and a white sweatshirt, stood by the fire, waving a wooden spoon as she directed the arrangement of ice chests and bags of food. Kids were spreading towels and blankets on the sand. Three guys and a girl flipped a Frisbee back and forth. There was music, laughter, and talk, good talk, and the pleasant summer smell of wood smoke carried on the onshore breeze.

They don't know I'm damaged goods.

The Frisbee went wild, tipped high by one of the guys, arcing out and then heading back for the fire. Deanna reached out and caught it neatly. Another girl – Jane couldn't quite remember her name – jumped to her feet and clapped once before holding out her hands, palm forward, the international signal for "Throw it to me," and Deanna zipped the orange disc to her. It turned into a laughing game of Keep Away, boys versus girls. The girl with the guitar quit; a transistor radio started playing "Incense and Peppermint."

One of the guys made a diving catch, rolled in the sand, looked up, and saw her. "Hey, there's Jane."

Deanna looked up, shading her eyes, and said, "Tony, Chuck, go help with her stuff."

"Aw ... "

"She's got beer."

"Hot dog!" The guys jumped to their feet.

"No, beer."

"Deanna, that's awful!"

In a short while, the radio was playing the Electric Prunes' "I Had Too Much to Dream Last Night," and the Three D's were gathered around a large metal pot of something – presumably spaghetti and meat sauce – balanced on the edge of the cement fire ring, taking turns stirring it with a huge wooden spoon. The sun dropped toward Catalina, and the breeze died. The fire was crackling nicely and occasionally throwing embers across the cement ring. Deanna raised the spoon, and the three of them marched around the fire ring counterclockwise, chanting, "Double, double..."

They finished the performance to a round applause and shouts of "Let's eat!" A guy stood up, waved his beer can, and began, "I vill now tell you of ze vonders of ze Krebs Cycle ..." He quit when he was hit in the face with a wet towel and the towel-thrower shouted, "Down with chemistry majors!"

Deanna poked at the stuff in the pot and said, "Five minutes."

I'm having a good time. This is nice.

Jane was very popular when she displayed the liquor. The short guy named Rider, whom she remembered was junior varsity coxswain of the crew team, loaded it into an ice-filled cooler, pulled out two cans, plopped down next to her, and handed her one. She pulled off the pop-tab and dropped it inside the can.

"I heard a kid did that and the tab came out and went in his throat and he choked and died before they could get him to a hospital."

"Wow." She giggled and spilled a little beer on his stomach. He was about five foot two, lean and muscular, red hair parted on the left and down over his ears. He smiled often, but in between, when his face was at rest, there was something else, something grim.

"I heard it from a coxswain at last year's San Diego Regatta. He knew somebody who actually was there."

Jane put her hand on his arm and looked deeply into his eyes. "Rider, life is just full of risk, isn't it?"

The smile flashed. "It was horrible!" He took a swig of beer, and then his eyes widened. He clutched at his throat and started making gagging noises before his eyes rolled back in his head, and choking dramatically, he flopped back on the sand, twitching, all without spilling any of the beer. "Ack! Ack! Mouth to mouth! Quick!"

He opened one eye and looked up hopefully.

Jane giggled and applauded.

He sat up, took a long drink, and then blurted out, "I'm graduating in June."

"What's your major?"

"PE. I always thought I'd coach, you know? Now ..."

"What?"

"I got the letter." She knew what letter he meant. Everybody did. "1A."

"Oh, Rider, I'm sorry. What are you going to do?"

He finished his beer, crumpled the can, and said, "I don't ... I gotta drain the lizard. Will you be here when I get back?"

"Yeah, yeah, Rider, I'll be right here."

A few minutes later, he came back with two fresh cans. "My dad wants me to enlist. He says I'll get a better MOS – military specialty or some shit like that – if I volunteer."

"What about your mom?"

"She goes along with Dad, but I think she doesn't want me to go."

"What about you? What do you want?"

"Half a million. Half a million guys over there. How can I choke and wimp out?" An obvious jock – probably football – ran by, chasing the Frisbee and kicking sand. The jock dove for the disc and caught it, rolling and kicking more sand. Rider quickly slapped his palms over their beers. "Hey, you guys watch it." He started to get to his feet when they ignored him. Jane put a hand on his arm and shook her head. He settled back, but he still watched the jocks. "Two guys from my high school class went over, and they both got killed."

"I'm sorry."

"My mom says their folks took it hard, you know?" She nodded. He drained his beer. "Let's pig down some spaghetti."

Jane had planned ahead, wearing cut-offs and her new ochre CSULB sweatshirt over a two-piece bathing suit. Now she pulled off the sweatshirt, dropped the shorts, stowed both in her beach bag, and said, "I'm ready. Lead on." Rider stared and then whistled appreciatively. She grinned. "Down, boy."

Deanna, the organizer, was using a large metal ladle that looked suspiciously like it belonged in the cafeteria to scoop steaming pasta and meat sauce and the occasional reddish-brown lump that was probably a meatball, out of the pot plopping everything onto paper plates. Salad was serve yourself, with tongs jammed into the Tupperware bowl of romaine and sliced tomatoes. Wonder Bread with some unidentified yellow stuff smeared on it was in another bowl.

Rider and Jane got helpings of everything. Then, equipped with more beer, they went back to their spot and sat. Rider looked at his plate dubiously. Then he shrugged, picked up a piece of lettuce, and ate it. Jane grabbed a handful of spaghetti noodles and shoved them in her mouth. She wiped her hand on her stomach (no napkins at the pig party, of course), before picking up her beer. Rider grinned and followed her example. Soon they were laughing, gnawing on meatballs, seeing who could choke down the largest mouthful of pasta, and having a great time.

A grossly fat kid waddled up, snagged a dripping beer out of a cooler, and plopped down on the sand. Somebody yelled, "Call Cal Tech! That's a seven-oh for sure."

"Laugh if you want," the fat kid said, "but the kid made it. Obese!" He finished his beer and crumpled the can into his stomach. The other partiers applauded. Rider whispered, "Four-F."

Jane whispered, "Don't get between him and the spaghetti."

"You have pasta in your hair."

"Where?"

"Right . . . there." Rider pulled out the strand and ate it.

Around them, kids laughed, drank, and smeared food on each other. Some of them were even eating.

After the spaghetti was devoured down to a black layer covering the bottom of the pot, they attacked and demolished an enormous chocolate sheet cake. Then everybody raced to the water and splashed around, laughing. Somebody said the red tide was due later that night. Donna, the biology major, explained that it was an algal bloom, lots of little plant-like things in the water, and if there were enough, the sea actually turned red. "Dinoflagellates are– "

"I got a big flagellate right here," one guy called out.

"Not what I hear," Deanna said to universal laughter.

"Yeah, is that why you wear glasses?" another guy said.

I'm having a great time, and I've met a guy who seems really nice. What am I doing pretending to be some kind of fink? I don't even know what I'm looking for. Or what I'd do if I found something. He doesn't know about me. Damaged goods.

I killed a man.

Rider was really nice. After they waded out into the cool water and washed off their dinner, they both pulled on sweatshirts and pants, shorts for her, jeans for Rider. He took Jane's hand and walked with her down the beach, into the dark, where he slipped his hand around her waist and kissed her, gently at first and then firmly. She had to bend at the waist a little, but it was okay.

Walking back, he said, "I've got to go to San Diego tomorrow for a regatta. But I'd like to see you again. How about a movie next Friday? I hear *Wait Until Dark* is great."

"Girl on my wing saw it and said it kept her awake all night."

"We can see something else, anything you want."

She snuggled close to him as they got close to the fire. "Okay."

"Really?"

"Sure! But if some guy jumps out with a knife–"

"You'll go? Great! Friday night. I'll pick you up."

The party – deemed a success by all – was winding down. The last of the cake had been eaten, and the spaghetti pot given a cursory rinse in the surf before being stowed in the trunk of Deanna's car. The couples who had wandered off into the dark to make out had returned. One girl in a two-piece was kneeling by the water, retching. Rider nudged Jane and said, "One beer too many. The old finger-down-the-throat always works." Rider took the next-to-last ice chest up to the parking lot, where two guys carefully checked it for any remaining beer. Finding none, they sadly poured out the remaining ice and water and put it in the trunk of an old Chevy.

Two older guys in cut-off jeans and t-shirts, not from the dorm, strolled down from the parking lot. One of the newcomers was tall and skinny, with black-framed glasses and a face that had fought a losing battle with acne. The other was shorter, but still big enough. Both had hair down to their shoulders. The short one had an unlit cigarette stuck in the corner of his mouth. They nudged each other and looked at Jane. The tall one said, "Hey, got any beer?" The wind shifted, and Jane caught a wave of spicy aftershave. Most people wore no shoes or, at most, go-ahead sandals at the beach, but both of these guys had on shoes and socks, one with high tops that Jane recognized as Chuck Taylors and the other – the one with the cigarette – actually had on hard shoes, along with cut-offs and a t-shirt.

Deanna said, "I think the last of it got drunk. I'll look." She took the lid off the ice chest and peered inside. "Nope. Sorry, guys. I have a Tab." She lifted one end of the ice chest and poured out the water and the few remaining ice cubes. One pink can of Tab rolled out onto the sand. Deanna picked it up and brushed the sand off before holding it out to the one with the cigarette. He ignored her, staring at Jane.

Hard Shoes turned to Jane and said, "How about weed?"

Chuck Taylors said, "Yeah, got any grass?"

Jane said, "No." She heard car doors slam. Engines started. Cars drove away, and it got very quiet. A small wave whispered as it withdrew, and faintly, she heard a loudspeaker on the pier announce that the beach was closing in half an hour.

"No way, Jose." Deanna firmly closed the lid to the ice chest.

"What are you, chicken?"

"What's it to you? Anyway, I'm going to teach school. One dope bust, and that's over. And, the beach is closing. You guys need to go on."

The newcomers looked at each other. Hard Shoes said, "What, you don't like our company? Blondie does, don't you, blondie?"

His buddy, the taller guy in the Chuck Taylors, snickered. "Yeah, blondie digs us all right."

Cigarette shot a significant glance at Jane. "Manny."

"Yeah. I see her."

Jane said, "We're bailing. Party's over."

Chuck Taylors – *Manny, his name is Manny* – said, "Why don't you come with us, cutie?"

"Yeah, let's get it on." He looked at Deanna. "Bring your friend but lose the dwarf."

Lose the dwarf. Rider's up in the parking lot. They've been watching us. Jane realized everybody was gone. The sun was down, and the beach was almost completely deserted. *The tall one. His voice is familiar.* Her throat went dry, and for a moment, she thought she heard a breeze whispering over the sand, through the corn, no, over the sand, no, it wasn't there.

Chuck Taylors grabbed Jane's arm. "C'mon, baby. Party time." His friend with the wing tips had Deanna, holding both arms, twisting one up behind her back.

Jane smiled and said, "Let me get something," and when Chuck Taylors looked confused, she jerked her arm free. She bent as if to pick up her beach bag, but instead she snatched a two-foot piece of wood from the pile of unburned firewood and tapped the end against her palm. "Time for you boys to go."

"C'mon, honey, don't bring us down. You ain't gonna hit nobody with that. We just want to have a good time." Manny grinned, showing teeth that had needed serious orthodontia, and took a step toward her. He said to his buddy, "Blondie," and nodded at Jane.

"Yeah. What's your name, cutie?"

"Puddin' Tame. Last chance. Let her go."

The intruders looked at each other, and Manny jerked his chin at Jane. The shorter one nodded in agreement, still holding Deanna's arm painfully twisted up behind her back.

Jane said, "Let her go."

In truth, it was a standoff. If they let Deanna go and left, that was fine, but if they just stood there, Jane was not ready to simply step up and hit one of them with the piece of wood, which she now noticed was a piece of two-by-four with a crack down the middle.

"C'mon, Jane, you know you're not gonna hit anybody with that." While Deanna struggled, Manny stepped confidently toward Jane.

Her shoulders sagged. "You're right."

He grinned. Another step. She planted her feet, lunged, and jabbed him in the stomach with the end of the two-by-four. The results were all she hoped for and more. His mouth dropped open, all the air whooshed out of him, and he staggered back, bent over, clutching himself across the middle, gagging and choking. Deanna took the opportunity to jerk her arm free and slap Cigarette across the face.

Then Rider was there, and he didn't hesitate, didn't ask what was going on; he just punched Chuck Taylors in the face. The tall guy went down. His friend stepped toward Rider, but Jane kicked him behind the knee, and he went down, too. Deanna stood, wide-eyed, holding a piece of firewood, looking scared and determined. "Get out of here," she said. She waved the firewood in their direction. They clutched at their heads and stomachs before they got to their feet and stumbled off, muttering.

Jane and Rider watched the pair until they were out of sight, and then they walked Deanna to her car, loaded the last of the stuff, and went back to see if anything of theirs had been left. All they found was an empty polka-dotted Wonder Bread wrapper that Jane crumpled and tossed into a trash can. They were walking back across the sand back to the parking lot, across the sand, when Hard Shoes and Chuck Taylors stepped out from behind a car and stood in front of them. They had things in their hands, tire irons maybe. Jane didn't hang around to find out. "Run!" Rider nodded but stood for a moment before following her, grimly looking at the approaching thugs, fists clenched.

They sprinted back toward the water, Jane running flat out, Rider pacing her easily. Behind them, they could hear their assailants laughing and catcalling. Jane snapped a look over her shoulder and saw them jogging along, still laughing, while she and Rider were rapidly increasing the distance between them.

"Wait, Rider, wait."

"Catch our breath, it's okay."

"That's not it, it's – uh-oh. That."

She saw the reason the thugs hadn't been trying too hard to catch up. Two more had appeared out of the dark ahead of them. Both of the newcomers wore gray sweatshirts fashionably turned inside out. They didn't seem to be laughing, but they were grinning as if at a fine joke. One made kissing noises, and now they all did laugh. Their assailants had spread out, Manny and his friend between them and the parking lot, the new pair blocking escape to the north and south, herding them toward the water. They were taking their time, calling out clever witticisms like "Hey, Blondie, ditch the dwarf and come with us" and the ever-popular "Yoo-hoo, baby."

How did this get out of hand so quickly? Who are these guys?"

Rider said, "Oh, shit."

"Yeah, we're in trouble here."

"I'll keep 'em busy. You break for the parking lot."

"Very noble. No way."

He puffed up. "I'm not scared of them."

"Well, you should be."

"Get help. I can't fight four guys."

"We."

"What?"

"We can't fight four guys. Besides, I've got an idea." Jane was looking around, not sure what she was hoping to find. Whatever it was, it wasn't there.

The others had stopped about ten yards on each side of Jane and Rider and now stood, slapping their weapons against their palms, enjoying the moment, nudging each other, building themselves up to serious violence. She didn't need to look to see the first two were closer.

Jane said, "Take off your pants."

"Yeah, that'll do it. They'll think I'm crazy."

"Can you swim?"

"Varsity butterfly my senior year at North Tucson High. Go Gila Monsters."

"I'll take that as a yes." She looked up the beach over the shoulder of the thug to the south, in the direction of the pier and the lifeguard headquarters, and waved frantically. "Hey, right here! Help! Help!"

They all fell for it and looked over their shoulders. Jane stepped out of her pink plastic go-aheads, dropped her shorts, and ran for the water, "Come on!" Rider was next to her, hopping on one foot as he pulled off his jeans. "Come *on!*" He jerked his foot free, and they sprinted across wet sand to the water's edge. Then they stopped, frozen at the sight.

The waves were glowing as they broke, liquid fire in the night.

Everything turns, turns, and with it the sea. The tide had turned and brought the red tide: millions of phytoplankton causing the water to fluoresce blue-white whenever it was stirred up.

It was beautiful, eerie, and strange. But the thugs behind them were running now, yelling something.

"Go!" Jane left a bright wake as she ran in and pushed through luminescent foam.

Rider hesitated a moment. Then he dove in and surfaced in waist-deep water that shone in the night as it swirled around him, flowing back out to sea. "What about this stuff? Isn't it bad for you?"

"Like we have a choice? Come on!" She dove under another wave and surfaced in sparks. He shrugged and looked back at their pursuers, who had stopped at the water's edge.

Jane and Rider kept wading out.

The infamous Huntington Trench, formed by shore break and riptides eroding the sand, was waiting for them – one step, and the water was waist-deep, and the next, it was over their heads, and then another step, and it was shallow again. They dove under two more glowing waves and then were outside the break line, treading water and watching the beach. They could see dim figures moving back and forth, probably deciding what to do. They heard low conversation and then, "Hey, you two! Come in before you drown. Jane, come out of the water. We was just fooling around. We won't hurt you, honest."

"Yeah, right," they both said at once, and then they laughed.

It was beautiful and strange, swimming quietly, with every motion stirring up the phytoplankton and causing bright flashes, living constellations flaring into life and then fading. The slow swells moved them gently up and down. Out to sea, the only thing visible were the lights of an oil island, miles off the coast.

"Okay, Jane, what's happening here?"

"Well, we're swimming through an ocean full of possibly poisonous glowing microorganisms because, if we go back to the beach, there are four or more thugs with tire irons who want to do us bodily harm."

He gaped at her. "Is this shit really poisonous?"

"Yes, Rider, in fact, the movie *Horror of Party Beach* was really a documentary about what happens to people who swim in it."

He started to say something, and she splashed glowing seawater in his face. "Oh, don't get any in your mouth."

He sputtered, spat, and muttered, "I saw that on *Science Fiction Theater* when I was a kid. Not very scary." Rider rolled over and floated on his back. "I could have kept them busy while you got help."

She kicked hard, pushing up out of the water to get a better look at the beach. "Bad idea. What would Kirk and Spock do?"

He muttered, "When I turn into a monster, you're the first one I'm coming after."

She settled back and floated, conserving energy. "Really? After all we've meant to each other?"

"Monsters always kill blondes in bikinis. It's a rule."

She couldn't argue with such an obvious truth, so she kept floating, watching the beach whenever a swell lifted her. She saw something very odd, and then she realized what was happening.

Rider whispered, "Okay, for real. Will this work?"

"Oh, sure. Rider. I do this all the time when I get chased by psychos with tire irons."

"Sorry."

"They won't follow us into the water."

"Does it occur to you that they may know something we don't? And what if they just wait? We can't stay out here forever."

"Watch that lifeguard station."

"I don't – oh."

The wooden tower was moving, sliding north.

Of course, it really wasn't moving north; they were drifting south. "The current, the rip, is carrying us down the coast, toward the pier. They won't have a clue where we come out."

"*If* we get out. Jane, we're caught in a riptide!" Even though they weren't swimming, only treading water, they were visibly moving at a good pace, about like a brisk walk. The water was warmer than the air, but they were still getting cold.

"Relax, we'll be fine. I'm just sorry I have to ditch my new sweatshirt, but it's getting heavy."

She stopped treading water and sank as she pulled the sweatshirt off over her head. She came up gasping, let it go, and watched as it floated for a moment and then dropped out of sight into glowing foam. Rider snapped off an instant surface dive and came up clutching it.

"I got it."

"Oh, no, I can–"

"I bench twice my weight. No problem. If I get tired, I'll ditch it."

"Thanks."

"So, Jane, look, uh, would you really like–"

"What?"

"How long do you think we have to stay out here?"

"Till we're sure they're gone, but that's not what you were going to say."

"Never mind."

"What? Don't make me splash you with more poisonous plankton." They drifted into a bed of kelp. Jane grabbed long slimy strands, rolled onto her back, and growled as she draped them around her arms and shoulders and waved them at Rider.

"Well, uh, will you really go to a movie with me? If you're not doing anything, but, you know, you probably are."

"Why, Rider, back on the beach, it sounded like you were asking me out on a date. You haven't changed your mind?" Jane let go of the kelp strands, and they floated away.

"You know, well, yeah, I mean, no, I haven't changed my mind."

"I'd love–"

Mess you up. Damaged goods.

She forced herself. "I'd love to."

He heard the hesitation. Of course he did, because he was expecting it.

"It's okay, you know, it was just something that popped into my head."

The current was moving them faster now. The beach, what they could see of it, was empty.

Before she could think of a way to fix what she had said, they were approaching the pier.

Rider said, "The Huntington Pier was built in 1912. It's been destroyed by storms and rebuilt. Now it's 1,800 feet long, one of the longest in the country."

Jane said, "How do you know this stuff?"

"My mother wrote and got brochures when I got accepted at Long Beach. She said I needed to know about, uh, I don't remember. Stuff. Oh man, I don't . . . never mind. We'll be fine."

"Uh-oh."

Waves push water onto the beach; if there is sufficient time between waves, the water is all pulled out to sea as undertow. Undertow had made it easy for Jane and Rider to get outside the break line.

But if the waves are too big or have too short a period – come in to shore too quickly – then the excess water is trapped and flows parallel to the beach like a swift invisible river, a riptide. Eventually, the current erodes a deep spot, chewing a trough in the sandy bottom so the water can flow swiftly out to sea.

Jane and Rider had been in such a current, pulling them south, but near the pier, they found themselves in a place where the waters suddenly turned and headed oceanward. The beach was shrinking behind them as they were dragged inexorably out into deep, cold water.

Rider started thrashing toward the shore. Jane caught his shoulder. "Don't fight it," she gasped. "Swim at an angle and head for the pier."

"How do you know all this stuff?"

"Junior" – she sucked in a breath – "lifeguard back home."

Stroking as hard as they could, they gradually made a little progress. Jane could see they were getting closer to the pier, but not to the beach.

No, that was wrong. They were losing ground, still being pulled out to sea. All at once, she could see them swept past the final piling into the dark, where the cold would sap their strength and they would drown. *Alone in the dark. No, not alone.*

Already, she couldn't feel her feet, and she thought about asking Rider if he could feel his, but what good would it do? Her hands were numb as well. Every now and then, she would take a stroke, but it would be too weak, just an impotent flailing at the surface, and she'd get a mouthful of seawater. She hoped she was still kicking.

We have to get out of the water whether those guys are waiting for us or not. Eighteen hundred feet. That's more than a quarter-mile.

As she stroked and kicked and got another mouthful of water, she saw they were definitely not going to make it. And in the lifeguard station atop the pier, the lights were out.

She could hear the swells hiss as they pushed around the pilings, leaving iridescent ribbons pointing at the beach, and the hiss almost sounded like a breeze, a moving stream of air sliding through corn stalks, and it didn't seem as cold, but she was tired, so tired. She looked back and saw Rider reduced to a dog paddle. But he still clutched her sweatshirt.

Foam. Around the pillar.

Wait. The glowing water around the pillars wasn't moving. When a wave pushed against a piling, the foam constellations stayed close. "Just a little more, Rider. The current stops this side of the pier." *I hope.*

He choked, spat, and suddenly he was shouting. "Right! Big Ten! Do it! Ten strokes with all you've got. Do it!" She felt new energy, cheered by his voice. "Ten strokes! One, two . . ."

Side by side, exhausted and numb, they forced out one stroke and then another, and on the eighth stroke, they thrashed under the pier. "Wait, don't touch the piling," she gasped. "Barnacles."

"I'll chance it."

"No, no. You got my sweatshirt?"

"Stuffed it in my shorts before the Big Ten. Why? Oh, oh, I get it. Yeah, good one, good one."

With the sweatshirt protecting his hands, Rider hugged the barnacle-encrusted cement pillar. Jane clung to his shoulders as the swells, larger now, pushed at them. "Catch our breath." She flipped hair back out of her eyes. "What's a big–" She choked again.

"Big Ten. At the end of a race, the cox calls for ten strokes with all you've got."

She could only nod. After a moment spent simply hanging on and breathing, Jane said, "All right. We go in under the pier."

They waited for a swell before pushing off and moving closer to shore. Before the undertow, strong here, could pull them back out, they clutched the next pillar. Jane could see her hands on Rider's muscular shoulders, but she couldn't feel them. Three more moves, and their questing toes dragged across sandy bottom.

Rider held the barnacle-ripped sweatshirt in one hand and Jane's hand in the other. He started to say something when, with one step, the bottom was gone, and they were in over their heads again.

They came up choking. "Damn trench," he spat again. It glowed, but they didn't care – the novelty had worn off. Two more steps, and they could touch. This time, it was for real, and a minute later, they were sprawled on the still-warm sand.

The beach was quiet and deserted. No crazies were waiting for them. He squeezed water out of her sweatshirt and handed it to her.

Jane squirmed and then tugged a brown piece of kelp out of her bikini top and tossed it aside.

She reached out and solemnly shook his hand. "I'd like to thank you for a lovely evening."

Then they were both laughing hysterically. When they settled down, she said, "Rider, about that movie–"

"It's okay, really."

"No, it isn't. I'd love to. But as you can probably tell, I'm kind of messed up. Damaged goods."

"I have no idea what you're talking about. But it's okay, you know, I understand."

She shook her head. "You don't. You couldn't possibly. I hit that guy with a two-by-four!"

"Yeah, good one."

"I could have seriously injured him! I poked him in the stomach, hard! What if I'd, I'd ruptured his spleen or something?"

"So?"

"You really don't care?"

He looked honestly puzzled. "Why should I? Whatever happens is on him – he tried to drag you away." He picked up the kelp frond she had pulled out of her top and gently brushed the sand off of it. "Jane, I've been in fights before, and that's just the way it is. If somebody starts something, you have to fight back with everything you've got. Trust me on this, I know."

You have to fight back with everything you've got. I think he means it. He doesn't care about the things I've done.

"What time will you pick me up?" They looked at each other for a moment, sitting in the dim light under the pier.

He showed her the kelp. "I'm going to press this in a book and keep it forever."

They were laughing again when headlights swept over them and a yellow Jeep stopped as they got to their feet. "Are you two all right? We had a report of two people in the water, maybe caught in the rip."

Jane blurted out, "Some guys were chasing us."

"We went in the water to get away," Rider added.

The lifeguard looked doubtful. "You wanna call the cops? Can you identify these guys?"

They declined to call the police, so the lifeguard settled for giving them a ride back to the fire rings. On the way, he used his bullhorn to tell stragglers the beach was closed. They rode until they could see Rider's jeans and Jane's beach bag with her shorts next to it, which they collected. They waved thank you to the lifeguard, who still looked at them oddly, and ran for the parking lot.

Jane drove Rider across the nearly empty parking lot to his car. It seemed like an obvious precaution that turned out to be unnecessary. When she pulled up next to his Falcon, they both got out, and after an awkward moment staring at his feet, he gestured at her car and came up with "Cool wheels."

"Prince. I call him Prince because he's a Valiant."

"Oh, yeah, I get it." He turned to walk away.

"Rider, I killed a man. When I was twelve years old. You know that old movie *The Bad Seed*? Well, that's me." He stared at her. *He's trying to decide whether to believe me.*

He dropped his shoes, braced one hand on Prince's fender to pull his jeans on, hopping as he tugged them up and fastened the metal buttons at the fly and the waist. Then he looked down as he slid his bare feet into the sandals. *He's stalling, stuck for something to say.* She opened Prince's door and got in.

He rested both hands on the edge of the window. "Never heard of it. Pick you up at seven."

On the drive up PCH to Bellflower and back to the dorm – regularly checking the rearview mirror for Rider – Jane did some serious thinking. It was better than remembering the chase through the corn.

Two incidents. Hippies beating up Terry Griswald and hippies chasing me and Rider. So much for nonviolence.

I'm the common denominator.

Enough. I'm sick of guys jumping out of the corn – shadows – and yelling, "Boo!"

When she got inside, she took a quick shower, glad that Deanna wasn't back yet, and put on dry clothes. Then she used the pay phone in the lobby to call the police station and leave a message for Griswald. Next, she called the number Blank had written on her arm

"Yeah? A-I." From the background noise, it sounded like a bar or restaurant. She left another message. Last, she called the number Maggie Molyneaux had given her and said she was ready for her first BID meeting. The voice on the other end said, "Never use that name on the phone again. Give me the phone number where you are and hang up."

A moment later, the pay phone rang, and when she picked it up, Junior said, "Welcome. Half an hour. Parking lot. We love you."

"I need to get cleaned up. Forty-five minutes." Jane hung up without waiting for an answer.

Five minutes later, she was standing in deep shadow on the Alamitos side of the lot. Traffic was routed through the lot one-way, with the entrance on the Alamitos side and the exit on the Cerritos side, so she could see any car and its occupants before they pulled up in front of the girls' dorm.

Almost as soon as she was in position, a dusty blue VW Transporter van, looking like a loaf of bread with wheels, rolled slowly through the lot with Junior behind the wheel. The passenger seat was empty, but that didn't mean there weren't people in the back. The van drove past Alamitos, turned to the Cerritos side. Then it backed into the dark corner where the first thugs had pushed Terry Griswald's car, and stopped. The lights went out. The air-cooled motor kept running.

When the glowing dial on her Lady Timex showed half an hour had passed, Jane slipped into deeper shadows and crossed the space between the dorms on the grassy little hill at the end. Dew had fallen, and the grass was slippery.

She crept up on the van and opened the passenger door. "Hey, sailor. Looking for a good time?"

It was very satisfying. Junior jumped and then closed his eyes and sucked in a deep breath, then another. "Don't ever, ever do that again."

Jane smiled and climbed up into the passenger seat after carefully looking in the back and seeing no one. "We can go now."

They drove down Bellflower, past the Bob's Big Boy where she and Terry Griswald had eaten burgers after the parking lot attack.

At the entrance to the Los Altos Drive-In, Junior held out his hand and gestured at her purse. Jane shook her head. He sighed and paid the requisite two dollars and pulled in for the midnight showing of *Slippery When Wet* and *Surf Crazy*. He parked in the next-to-last row, next to another, even-more-battered windowless Corvair van. "Go."

The side door opened, and Jane saw the three girls plus Maggie were crowded into open space behind the two front buckets. There were no rear seats.

They're all here. She hesitated. *Well, this is what I came for.* She climbed in.

Andromeda raised a bota bag, expertly took a long squirt, and passed it to her. Jane shook her head and handed it into the back.

Junior climbed in and took the driver's seat, turning sideways and resting one arm on the seatback. He said, "Ceres, you are Jane's sister, having found her. You brought her to us out of love?"

"Yes. Out of love." Maggie – Jane couldn't get into the space names – went on. "Okay, we think Jane might be one of us. We'll find out. Jane, do you believe the establishment is evil, that the war is wrong?"

"Yes."

"And it must be stopped by any means necessary? And as part of the family both bound and freed by our undying love, do you agree wholeheartedly that you are obligated to help us in any way you can?"

When did I become a member of the family?

Maggie paused, clearly expecting a response. Jane said, "I used to not think so, you know? I thought peaceful protest could make a difference. Now, well, now it hasn't worked, so I guess it's anything goes. We gotta stop it."

Maggie looked at her for a moment. Then she looked at Junior, where who sat behind the wheel, staring at her and smoking, before she said. "That's not exactly the kind of commitment BID needs." Jane shrugged. "But I guess it will do for now. Everything we do, we do out of love."

The others echoed, chanting, "Out of love. Out of love. Out of love." They all looked in her eyes and then moved so they could touch her, placing hands on her shoulders, her arms, her hands, and Jane found herself almost joining them, her lips starting to form the words of the chant. It was that powerful.

Junior grunted. "Okay, here's the plan. We need money. We want you to find out which of those richos you're hanging with has the most money – they're all Newport Beach parasites – and then we're gonna grab her. Her parents will pay to get the little princess back."

This was not what Jane had expected. She opened her mouth to say so, but Junior continued. "Hey, we won't even have to hurt the little darling, and her parasite father won't even miss the money. And we need it." Jane just looked at him.

Andromeda nodded and smiled. "Parasites. All of them. Cute plastic Barbies. Never had to learn to cook."

How much do they know about me? While I was trying to get close to Maggie, was she doing the same to me? Was that why it was easy? How serious is this mistake?

Pleiades, looking even more like a praying mantis with the images from the movie reflecting off her glasses, put her hand over Jane's. "Out of love. We love you." Then she smiled, showing teeth, before she got out, and she and Junior went back to his van.

All she could think was: *They assume I'm ready to help them kidnap one of my friends.*

On the screen, bodysurfers were getting destroyed by huge waves. The speaker, hooked to the driver's-side window, screamed, "Wipeout! Taking gas at the dirty, nasty Newport Beach Wedge!"

Large Andromeda drove the Corvair van with the small girl who never spoke, Maggie Molyneaux, and Jane back to the dorm.

The Second Nightmare

He's gaining.

One chance. She knew it was weird to imagine things when you were dreaming, but she did. She saw herself at twelve years old, running across the dirt road that bordered the cornfield and slipping down behind a pile of irrigation pipes and hiding. She saw him leaving in frustration. In the way they have, the dream showed her that hope and then showed her that it would not, could not, happen. Then she was in the corn.

He's gaining.

She jumped across the boards covering the dry well, touching only with one light, twelve-year-old foot. He thundered after her, stepped on the boards, hesitated as he heard the cracking sound, and threw his arms out, but the boards gave way, and he pitched forward as he went down. He caught lumber on the far side of the opening and clutched desperately. Then it gave way and slid down into the dark. He caught the cement rim. One of the boards must have had a nail in it, because he had a cut running down from his hair and sliding across his left ear. Blood ran down his neck and into the collar of his once-white shirt. When his fingers slipped, she could see the streaks of blood where the rough cement had shredded his fingertips, which was weird because it was so dark she shouldn't have been able to see anything, but it was a dream, and she knew it was a dream. The wind stopped, and the only sound in the night was his ragged breathing. Then somewhere a bullfrog harrumphed, and the corn whispered, perhaps answering the frog, perhaps asking what she would do, perhaps indifferent to it all.

He looked up, eyes wide and staring, face white in the moonlight except where it was covered with black blood.

"Hey, kid, please. Please help me. I'm sorry. Pull me up, okay? I won't hurt you, I promise." He lunged and caught more of the edge. She sat in the dirt, folded her hands in her lap, and just looked at him. His face changed. "You little bitch. When I get out of here, I'm going to mess you up. Like your folks. Worse." He had a forearm out now. He clawed. He muttered, "Mess you up, mess you up," over and over.

She'd fallen when she'd made the jump, and she'd scraped her forehead. She felt the blood running down onto her shoulder and thought, *We both have bloody faces. Mommy won't be mad.*

In the dream, the drizzle turned to hard rain, but for some reason, it didn't wash away the blood running down her face. His eyes widened as he realized he was losing his grip. Still, she watched. "I was kidding, okay? I didn't mean it. C'mon, kid, you don't want to do this. Please. Please!" His hands slipped, first the left, then the right. He scrabbled with his right hand. The index fingernail broke off, and the blood looked black in the moonlight.

Jump cut. This was a dream.

The nail snapped off his index finger again. He fell. He screamed as he fell. There was a thud, and then the only sound was the corn, the whispering corn, and her breathing. The rain stopped. Blood dripped off her chin. She ran.

Jump cut.

He's gaining. He really is getting closer. What happens when he catches me?

And suddenly she knew he was back there. He'd crawled up out of the old well, broken and bleeding and grinning. There was blood on his chin, in his teeth. In the dream, she wondered if he could taste the blood. "That's right," he said. "You're just like me." And he was behind her in the dark, between the corn rows, but she knew what his face would look like, bloody and grinning around broken, bloody teeth. She could hear him. "Mess you up. Mess you up, you little bitch." He was right behind her. She tripped and threw out her hands. *This is where I always wake up.*

His bloody hand closed around her ankle.

She woke up.

Across the room, Deanna snored gently.

Jane and Junior

On Friday, Rider was in the Cerritos lobby at seven in white Rayon bellbottoms and a striped Hang-Ten t-shirt. They walked to his battered but clean Ford Falcon station wagon. The engine sounded good, but the brakes required pumping before they deigned to stop the car. The movie – they did go to *Wait Until Dark* – was scary, especially the end, and everybody in the theater screamed at the very last knife attack. On the way back to the dorm, he talked about the crew team's race tomorrow.

Monday, walking past the bookstore on her way to LH-151, Jane saw Maggie seated on one of the cement benches bordering the patio. Maggie jerked her head, toward the bookstore. Jane followed her to a rear corner of the store, where the tall girl nervously pushed her hair back as she pretended to look at shelves of history texts.

Jane said, "What? I've got a ten o'clock." Seeing the look on Maggie's face, she went on. "Yeah, I know, come the revolution, my GPA won't matter, but for now, it does."

"I don't like your attitude."

"You're not really going to kidnap one of my friends, are you?"

Maggie looked over her shoulder, but the kids around them seemed more interested in pricing used books than overhearing criminal plans. She pulled Jane further into the corner.

"We need the money for Junior's plan. Are you in or not?"

"Come back with a real plan and I'll let you know."

"Come with me."

Jane, now concerned for Deanna, nodded and followed Maggie up the hill to *Anonymous*, where the other members of BID were gathered in the shade of the enormous wooden sculpture. It looked like they were both cutting class.

Junior repeated the plan. Jane again said no way.

Junior looked at Andromeda. The big girl smiled and said, "You were right. You're always right."

He said, "Well, if we can't get one of them, we'll take you."

Maggie said, "Junior, we need to think about this, you know?"

"Bullshit. What we gotta do is snatch her, get the money, and make the buy."

"Kidnapping's serious." Jane was glad to hear Maggie Molyneaux sounding surprised.

Too late, Jane was edging toward the walk. Junior and Andromeda grabbed her. He said, "Okay, dig this. We call your folks, say if they want to see your blonde curls again they cough up a cool hundred grand."

"You're crazy."

"It'll work. And the best part is you're one of us, so nobody will believe you if you try to say we kidnapped you." He held one arm while Andromeda held the other.

Maggie said, "Jane, listen, nobody gets hurt, okay? Your folks can afford it, we need the money, and of course, we'd never really hurt you." But Maggie looked at Junior when she said the last. Junior grinned.

That answered Jane's questions about why BID had been so easy to penetrate.

"I gotta think about this, okay? My folks are old, and they're not very well. This could do real damage." She saw his face. *They really know. They know my folks are rich. Stall. Stall for time.* "How did you know?"

With his free hand, Junior reached up under his sweatshirt and scratched his stomach. "The family is powerful. We have many resources, many friends."

"Messing up the establishment is one thing, scaring a couple of sick old people who never hurt anybody in their lives is another. No, this is a stupid idea. I'm out."

Junior pulled her close to his musty jacket. Andromeda moved with her, staying close. His moustache tickled as he whispered in her ear, "Jane, we love you."

The others – except Maggie – echoed, "Love you."

He pulled her closer, still looking up at her and grinning. Again, Andromeda moved with him, but Jane thought her grip was a little bit looser. "To everything, there is a season, the eternal cycles, you dig? Now it's our time, and I know it's not easy, but the needs of the family are more important than the individual, and always remember, they got the guns. We got the numbers, so we have to fight any way we can. You'll understand more in a while." He nodded at Andromeda, who twisted Jane's arm up behind her back. Jane winced. Junior nodded at Andromeda. "She'll be more convincing when she makes the call."

Andromeda whispered, "I bet they never told you it was snowing down south or you needed to learn to cook."

"What? Cook? What on earth are you talking about?"

Andromeda murmured, "Junior's right. He's always right." They all nodded, even Maggie.

"Oh, all right." Jane sagged. "I understand." Junior looked almost disappointed, but he relaxed. Then Jane kicked him in the shin as hard as she could, glad that her penny loafers had a hard sole. He let go, and she elbowed Andromeda in the stomach before she ran, not bothering to look back, pretty sure that they wouldn't try to catch her with thousands of kids around.

Jane and Rider

Then Rider was running next to her, matching her pace easily. He looked back over his shoulder. "Are people always chasing you?"

Well, as a matter of fact, they are. But I'm used to it. Except I don't like the corn. No, I don't like the corn at all.

"What are you doing here?" He didn't answer. "Rider–"

"Okay, okay. I was following you. I saw you walking up the hill and thought you might like to hang out before lunch, but then you were sitting with those BID freaks, and then that guy and the big girl–"

"Andromeda."

"–grabbed you. You want me to go back and pound him?"

"No, but I guess we should get my books. Hope they're still there."

The members of BID were gone, but the books were there on the grass, *Elements of Modern Health* lying on top of the stack.

Rider trotted over and picked them up, dusted a few leaves of grass off of *Writing with a Purpose*, her English comp text, and handed them to her. Then, before she could take them, he pulled them back and said, "I'll carry 'em. If you want. I mean, if that's okay." He blushed almost as red as his hair.

Jane grinned and slipped her arm through his. "Why, thank you, kind sir." Her pleasant musings were cut short when Junior appeared in front of them. He ignored Rider.

"That hurt. When you kicked me, it hurt."

Rider stepped between them and said, "Naw, that didn't hurt. But I can show you hurt if you want." He smiled as he looked Junior in the eye. He had to look up to do it.

"Yeah, right."

"Anytime." Rider's voice was soft. "Anytime at all."

According to his elementary school teachers, Rider had a chip on his shoulder. Always ready to fight, by the time he was a junior in high school, he'd had the scarred knuckles to prove it. He smiled at Junior. It was not a pleasant smile, rather a toothy grimace that said he simply didn't care; he would fight till he couldn't stand and then get up and fight more. That had gotten him through life on the playground. Around them, kids moved, the river of students, all carrying books, flowing from Lower Campus to Upper Campus and back again, from parking lot to lecture hall to lab to library and back to parking lot. None of them seemed to notice the open hostility on Junior's face. Without taking his eyes off Junior, Rider handed Jane her books.

Junior shoved his hands in the pockets of his Army field jacket and walked away.

Rider watched him go.

Jane swallowed. "Thanks."

Rider grinned. "You never introduced me to your friend."

They started walking again. "His name's Junior, and he's sort of a, you know, friend of a friend."

"He looks like a hippie radical. How much do you know about him?"

"Not much. Always wears a 'Make Love Not War' button." *But he knows about me.*

"Yeah, right. What's his last name?"

"No idea. Why do you care?"

Suddenly he looked cautious. "No reason, except he looks like somebody to watch out for."

At the cafeteria, before Rider went inside to drink coffee with his crew team buddies and Jane headed down to the dorm, he put his hand on her arm at the door and then pulled it back.

"Jane, listen, you be careful, okay?" he said, just above a whisper. "I know guys like Junior, I've dealt with them all my life, and he's not done. You watch out, all right? Promise?"

Solemnly she said, "Yes, sir, I promise." Then, on impulse, she kissed his cheek. She had a split second of doubt – *Bend at the waist or knees, which will be less bad for him?* – and decided on waist.

For a moment, he stared at her, grinning and happy. He started to say something. Then he shook his head and went into the cafeteria.

That night at dinner, Rider sat with her, Deanna, and the other girls from Jane's wing. After chocolate chip ice cream, they played Drop the Penny. Dampen the rim of a glass, stretch a paper napkin over the rim, and place a penny in the center of the napkin. The object of the game: use a lit cigarette to burn a hole – the smaller the better – in the napkin without causing the penny to fall through. Of course, the more holes there are, the more difficult it gets. Rider didn't smoke – he had to borrow cigarettes – nevertheless, he was the undisputed champion. But that night, he lost three games in a row. He stalked off to calls of "Choke! Choke!"

Jane hurried down the hill after him, dumped her books in her room, and went across the parking lot to Los Alamitos. When Rider came down the stairs, she took his hand and led him to a couch in the corner of the common room.

"Okay, Rider, what's happening?"

He let go of her hand, hesitated, and then took it back. "Jane, you know I care about you." *He's going to tell me there's someone else.* To her surprise, the thought produced only a mild sadness, the kind you feel when you clean out your room at the end of the school year, packing up books and clothes, rolling up posters, thinking about summer and the next semester.

"Let's walk." He took her hand and led her out the front door and up the steps to the parking lot. They strolled up to State College Drive, where the peach trees were showing tiny dormant buds, waiting for the season to change. They walked past the Soroptomist House, where Jane had attended Freshman Orientation. He was silent, holding her hand, looking straight ahead.

"Rider, just spit it out, okay? Just say whatever it is. C'mon, I saved you from the tire iron thugs and the poisonous glowing goo."

He let go of her hand and stared. "You what? Hey, I–" Then he saw her expression. "Got me again."

She took his arm and started them walking again. "Talk, big boy." As soon as the words passed her lips, she regretted them. He looked at her for a moment, eyes wide, hurt. Then he sort of grinned. She squeezed his bicep.

"Yeah, sure. Look, I'm not supposed to do this, but I care about you, and, and it's not fair to not tell you."

"Rider . . ." she said, "who is she?" just as he blurted out, "I'm not just a student."

She looked at him. "Look, if you have a girlfriend back home, just tell me." *You'd be better off. I'm damaged goods.*

His jaw dropped. "What? A girlfriend? No, that's not it. I'm working with the government. I can't tell you very much, I'm not supposed to say anything, but I can't go on lying to you." He looked around before whispering, "First, I have a question. This girl named Maggie. How well do you know her?"

I missed it. ". . .sitting with those BID freaks." He called Junior's family BID, and I'd never told him.

"What do you mean, working for the government? Like, the post office or something?" Even as she said it, she knew the answer, but things were spinning out of control, and she had to stall for time. For some reason, she thought about playing in the corn field when she was a little girl. *Before the bad man came. Before safe houses and a new school every year. Sometimes every semester.*

"She's tall, really good looking, always wears this field jacket with lots of anti-war buttons."

"I'm not sure who you mean." That seemed safe for now, and it was sort of true. There could be more than one Maggie.

"C'mon, Jane, I saw you talking to her. Look, I'll be straight with you. You need to stay away from her."

"Why? If it's who I think you're talking about, she's in my health ed class."

"I know. Jane, please." He paused, seeming to think about how much to say. "She's dangerous, part of a dangerous group called Burn It Down, BID. I know you don't want to have anything to do with people like that, so just stay away, okay? It's for your own good."

Why, gee, Rider, there's something we have in common. I'm spying on kids too. But she didn't say it. She remembered what she had been taught, the man in the suit telling her: "Even if you get caught, look 'em in the eye and lie. Your life, and others, might well depend on it."

The real question was not whether to confess to Rider but whether to make a call and report the contact to Terry Griswald and Wingarten. Or she could call the men in suits.

They were almost up the hill to the bookstore. He had her hand again, only now he was squeezing it hard. "Please don't be mad. I'm not really a snitch. I mean, well, yeah, no, I guess I am. Don't be mad."

"Tell me about this CI stuff."

"Yeah, CI . . . Wait, how do you know that?"

"Must have read it somewhere. Maybe TV. Confidential informant, right?" *Mistake! He hadn't said the words "confidential informant," much less the initials.*

"Well, you know my family lives in Tucson."

"Yeah."

"Okay, well, the government's helping with my out-of-state fees. In return, I keep my eyes open. It's no big deal. Really."

"Why are you telling me?"

He looked at her, open-mouthed. "Why? Well, like I said, I don't want to lie to you."

"But isn't it dangerous to tell me the truth?"

"Oh, Jane, I trust you completely."

Well, that's your first mistake. "Rider, promise me you won't say anything to anybody else. No one at all."

"Oh sure, absolutely. Not even the guys on the team know."

"Good. Keep it that way. Rider, that includes telling your handler that you told me. They would be very upset." *Shit. "Handler." Will he catch it?*

He didn't. "Look, there's something else, okay?" *Here it comes.*

In the early evening, the campus was quiet, a few people walking to their cars, noise coming from the fraternity section of the cafeteria. They crossed the quad and sat on the grass by the metal sculpture called *Mu 996*, which was sort of an enormous lopsided metal toadstool with carvings in its side. The shadow stretched away from them.

"What?"

"Has she told you about anything they're planning?"

"Who?"

"Come on, Jane, this is serious. Maggie, I don't know her last name, and the others in BID, it means–"

"Burn It Down. You told me." *He did mention the name, right? I really, really wish I was better at this stuff.*

She hurried to cover the possible mistake. "And no, I don't think it's really real, just something they talk about." As she said it, Jane thought, *That's true, isn't it? These kids are basically harmless. They talked about kidnapping but backed down almost at once.* "I know they're going to the demonstration next week. At least, I think so."

"What about you?"

"Yeah, probably. I've got a term paper due, but it should be finished by then. I gotta say, the war sucks. I just don't think blowing up buildings is gonna help, you know?" When she'd said that to Maggie, the tall girl had stared at her and said, "You have a term paper? Jane, people are dying and all you care about is a term paper?" The only answer Jane had been able think of was yes, but she hadn't said it. Now Rider was saying it to her.

Rider stood, stuck out a hand, and pulled her to her feet. Jane went into the cafeteria for a cup of tea and a chance to think while Rider headed back down to the dorm. Reviewing Rider's confession, she noted that he had not said what agency had recruited him, only "the government." *Was he telling the truth? Yes, no question.* He didn't need to make up a story like that to impress her, and if he had, it would have been more polished. Was there a possibility that Captain Wingarten, or Thaddeus Blank, had two informants working on BID? Would either of them tell her if there was another one? Yes, and not necessarily. She hadn't told Rider she was a CI. What to do? Oh, and there was the minor issue that Rider was getting paid and she wasn't. The smart thing to do would obviously be to call in and resign. Then tell Maggie she was done playing revolutionary, wish her well, and get back to health ed and poli sci and English literature to 1500. There was one compelling reason not to.

Jane was having a good time, perhaps the best time of her life. It didn't take her long to decide what to do.

The next day at lunch – it was Make Your Own Sandwich Day – Jane appeared next to Rider as he sat with a plate of sandwiches and said, "We need to talk." He heard the words and jumped. "No, not that kind of talk. I'm one too." She took his arm and guided him away from the tables. He was still eating the last half of his baloney-and-cheese as they exited.

"One what?" Then he got it, and his eyes widened, and he stepped back so he didn't have to look up at her.

"Yeah. Long Beach Police." *And they're reporting to some other men in suits, but you're not ready for that.*

He just stared at her.

"I'm not narcing on anybody, really. They just wanted me to keep my eyes open." Even as the words came out, she realized how much she sounded like Rider. Jane took a deep breath. "And I sort of owed them." Rider was still staring at her, open-mouthed. "C'mon, say something, will you? I know you're mad, and I don't blame you."

"And they asked you to check up on me at the beach party, and that's why–" He stopped, and she could see the hurt in his eyes.

She said, "Who?"

"What?"

"Later. No, I was not spying on you at the pig party. No way. Geez."

He blurted out, "Well, they asked *me* to check up on *you*." Now it was her turn to be surprised. "I tried to tell you at the beach party, but then those guys came."

Suddenly they were both talking at once.

"Oh my god!"

"What, I mean, how did you–"

"–get started–"

"Who approached–"

Then they were both laughing, and she knew it was going to be all right. She was laughing so hard tears were streaming down her face, and she held on to his arm as they passed the bookstore. He was looking around, studying the crowds.

Jane said, "I don't see any BID kids."

"I was looking for somebody I know." For a minute, she didn't get it. Then she giggled and snuggled closer. He flushed. "Well, I wish some of the guys could see us. You. Me with you." They started laughing again.

Finally, Jane held up both hands. "Okay, geez, stop before I wet my pants."

She rummaged in her macramé purse and pulled out a tissue, blew her nose, and started laughing again. She controlled it with difficulty.

He said, "One of us at a time."

She said, "Pants-wetting?" And they both were laughing again. She nodded. "You first." When he didn't say anything, she went on. "Rider, there are some things you don't know about me."

"I don't care."

She sighed. "Okay, later for that."

"And they really didn't ask you to check up on me at the beach party?"

"No!

"Well, like I said, they asked me to check up on you."

"What? Oh man. Yeah, you said that, didn't you?"

"So the people who are using us aren't telling us everything. Okay, look, what are we going to do?"

Still frowning, she said, "The cops have both of us spying on Burn It Down, but those kids seem pretty harmless to me. I mean, they talk about doing stuff, but I don't think they'll follow through. Do you?"

"Uh, well, actually I haven't talked to any of them. I couldn't figure out how to."

"You've met Junior, and you two really got along."

"Yeah, we hit it off." Rider grinned.

Jane rolled her eyes. "He is a real creepy guy. Seems like he's got this sort of harem, girls that hang around him. The one I know best is that girl named Maggie. I think right now she's in a class in FA-1 that gets out in a half hour. Let's go up and talk to her."

He grinned. "And say what? 'Hey, are you crazies planning to do something bad?'"

"We'll think of something on the way."

Reluctantly, he said, "Why don't we just call Wingarten and demand to know, you know, what's the deal?"

"You said the cops are paying your out-of-state fees? I think we better try to get some information before we rock the boat."

"Oh, that. Yeah, maybe you're right. You need to go to your room for books or anything?"

"Nope. Let's go."

Ten minutes later, they were standing on the cement patio outside Fine Arts-1. Two classrooms had doors propped open; from one came the drone of a lecture; in the other, students were hunched over Blue Books, either scribbling or staring blankly, waiting for exam inspiration. On the walk from the cafeteria, Jane had reconsidered. She was glad she hadn't told Rider everything, but she couldn't help feeling bad about holding out on him. "Look, I don't think she'll say anything if you're with me."

Obligingly, he moved over to the food machines and sat on a bench.

Class ended, and students started filing out of the rooms. For a moment, she wasn't sure they'd find the tall girl, but then Maggie appeared with the last of the crowd, clutching her books to her chest. Jane almost missed her because the Army field jacket was gone, replaced by a white long-sleeved blouse, an unbuttoned pale green cardigan, and a short green plaid skirt.

She walked past Jane with her head down, long hair shrouding her face. Jane fell in beside her. "Hey, I almost didn't recognize you out of uniform." Maggie kept walking, with Rider a pace behind and on Jane's left. "Listen, I need to talk to you." Maggie shook her head and didn't slow, still hunched over her books. They passed the nine-story Humanities Office Building and approached the u-shaped turnaround that was for very short-term parking and visitor drop-off. "It's important and–" Something in the way the tall girl kept looking down made Jane step in front of her, forcing her to stop. "Hey! Look, I–" Maggie Molyneaux looked up, and Jane involuntarily took a step back. "Oh my god! Maggie, what happened? Who did this to you?" *As if I didn't know.*

Maggie's left eye was swollen almost shut; a large purple bruise covered that cheek, and there was a raw scrape down low, at the edge of her jaw. Jane thought, *A ring did that. Somebody hit her, and the ring scraped her face.*

"Was it Junior?" Maggie shook her head and started to sniffle. Now Rider was standing in front of them. He looked at Maggie and let out a low whistle.

"I fell. Off my bike. I fell."

Rider glanced at Jane and then back at Maggie. "Maggie, my name's Rider. I live in Alamitos. I've seen you around, okay? And I've seen bruises like that. In the mirror."

"I fell. I was just going down the driveway, and I must have hit a rock or something, and, and then I went over the handlebars."

He pulled her left hand free of her books, gently took her wrist, and turned her hand palm up. "How come your hands aren't scraped? You take gas off a bike, you always throw out your hands to break the fall."

Jane couldn't stop staring. "Maggie, who was it? Was it Junior?"

"No."

Still gentle, Rider slid her sleeve up. Her forearm was marked with new purple bruises. He looked at Jane and shook his head.

Something clicked for Jane. "It was the girls. Junior's little family."

The tall girl seemed to wilt. Head down, she nodded. "Pleiades and Tranquility held me. Andromeda hit me. She's big, and she's really strong. Then she held me, and the others hit me. They, they took turns."

"Why? Was it because of me?" *Of course it was.*

They heard the VW van coming before it rattled to a stop behind them, and the three girls got out and stood by the door. Maggie turned toward them, wincing as Rider held on to her bruised arm. Jane said, "Maggie, what are you doing? Are you nuts? Don't go with them!"

"I like you, Jane, I really do. But I love them. They're my family. I have to go. They love me. I was wrong. I messed up, and I needed a lesson. Our love makes us strong. I'm stronger now. I have to go."

Jane and Rider looked at each other. Short of grabbing her, there was nothing they could do. Rider let go of her arm and raised his hands in an "I give up" motion. After a last look at Jane, Maggie shook her head, clutched her books tighter, and trotted over to the van. One after another, the girls all hugged her, Andromeda looking over Maggie's shoulder at Jane as she did, looking over Maggie's shoulder and smiling. Maggie got in the van. Pleiades and the one Jane thought of as Nowhere Girl – Tranquility, that was her family name – got in after her. Andromeda stared at Jane and Rider for a moment, still smiling. Then she got in and slammed the door shut.

Jane and Maggie

After dinner – burgers and fries – and another round of Drop the Penny, Jane and the Three D's strolled back to the dorm, where Jane saw Maggie standing in the Cerritos common room, nervous, twitchy, licking her lips. Bruised. Wearing the field jacket again, over jeans and a striped blouse. Jane started to walk past.

Maggie licked her lips and said, "Please, hear me out, okay?" Jane stopped and said, "It's your dime." The D's waved and continued on up the stairs.

This is better than I thought. I don't need to find a way to get back in touch.

After Maggie had left in Junior's van, Jane and Rider had decided to give it a couple of days and then go to Griswald and/or Wingarten. Maggie's beating had made it serious. Privately Jane thought she'd have to find a way to talk to the members of BID. She hadn't told Rider. And now, here was Maggie, urgently wanting to talk.

Of course, it's probably a trap. They might still want to "kidnap" me. Only one way to find out.

Maggie sat on one end of a couch in the common room. "Please." Jane didn't sit next to her, just gave a curt nod. "I'm sorry, really sorry, okay? About the kidnapping thing, you know? I knew Junior was, uh, pretty–"

"He's nuts. Let's review in case there's a quiz. He grabbed you in the cafeteria. He grabbed me and threatened to kidnap me to extort money from my parents. And – here's the big one, class – he had his three trained harpies beat the crap out of you. Are you taking notes? You should be."

"No, no, really, you just, you just, have to understand that he's really committed to the cause, and so are the girls, and they got carried away. Junior was really mad at them for hitting me. Really mad."

Jane shook her head. "No, Maggie, he likes it. He was having a good time when he grabbed me. I repeat: he likes it."

All at once, Jane stopped talking and stared into the distance.

I've met somebody else who liked it. I didn't see it at first, but it's true. Blank. Thaddeus Blank likes hurting people, maybe even more than Junior does. He calls his razor, what? 'Miss Telstar.' Oh man. How could I miss it?

Miserably, the tall girl said, "We just really needed the money. Junior says this is the most important thing we'll ever do. This will change everything. But it's okay. We got . . . enough . . . and we don't need it anymore. That's what I wanted to tell you. It's ok. We don't need it anymore."

"What do you need it for?"

Maggie just shook her head. Jane turned away.

"Wait, I–"

"You either trust me, or you don't." *And you're a fool if you do, honey.* "Maggie, listen, has Junior ever talked about a guy named Thaddeus Blank?"

"No."

"Wears a suit, carries a straight razor, and–"

That was all it took. The tall girl's dark eye that wasn't swollen widened before she shook her head and muttered, "We have this plan, something big."

"Oh, good. It's important to have a plan."

"I can't talk about it in here. Walk outside with me."

"Let's not and say we did."

Maggie flushed. "All right, I don't blame you for that. How about I give you my word?"

"How about Mr. Chock-Full-O-Nuts? Will he give his word?"

"Just to the top of the steps. Please."

Jane nodded, and they walked past the reception desk, a counter with a glass partition separating the switchboard and the open side of the mailboxes. Jane made sure she waved at the student assistant on duty, pretending to recognize her, and said, "I'll be right back if anybody's looking for me." The girl looked up from a much-thumbed copy of *Valley of the Dolls* long enough to nod.

Outside, they stood at the top of the stairs in the cool evening, looking out toward Los Alamitos Hall and, to the left, the open field where Jane had first run from the police and where she had gotten her forehead sliced. Absently, she reached up and touched the spot. "Okay, Maggie. Look, you seem okay, but some of your friends, wow, I don't know."

"It's changing."

"What's changing?"

"The world, Jane, everything. Can't you feel it? In France, students shut down almost every university. It's the world, Jane. They got the guns; we got the numbers. Youth, Jane, we're taking over. We're taking over with love, and it's all going to be better, and we're part of it. You can be too. I, I like you, Jane, and I know you are new to The Movement and to Junior's Vision" – the way the tall girl said it, Jane could hear the capital letters – "but you'll fit right in, and, and . . ." Suddenly she blurted out, "Don't you want to do something with your life? Something important?"

"Yeah, I want to finish my term paper."

"I got a joint. You wanna go smoke it with me?"

"Term paper."

"You wanna help, right?"

"Sure! Maybe Andromeda and her pals will beat the crap out of me too."

Maggie smiled weakly. "You said there would be a quiz. Look, you wanted to know what we needed the money for."

"Honey, this is where I came in, you know?" *Should I start to go back inside? No. Let's push it.* "He wants to put drugs in the water, doesn't he?"

Maggie leaned forward, her long, straight hair brushing Jane's shoulder. The tall girl swallowed hard and nodded.

"What stuff?"

"Can't tell you that yet."

Acid. It has to be LSD in the water. Okay, I was wrong; they have a real plan. Jane's eyes were drawn to the water towers across the street.

"Okay, how?"

"I *really* can't tell you that."

Maggie grabbed Jane's arm as Junior's van turned into the parking lot, puttered to the far end, and rolled to a stop. There was a very bad moment when Jane thought Andromeda and her friends would jump out and she'd be dragged into the van. Out of love, of course.

Instead, Maggie hustled Jane inside the doors, and then the tall girl stood looking out into the dark at the van, chewing her lower lip and absently brushing her hair forward to cover her bruises. "I gotta split. I gotta split. Listen, Jane, don't tell Junior I told you about this, please, please. He really, really wouldn't like it."

"I doubt that I'll be having many conversations with Mr. Grab-My-Arm, but sure, I won't tell him anything."

"Thanks, thanks. I gotta split," Maggie blurted out, and then she looked down at her Birkenstocks and added, "I want you to be with us." She turned toward the door.

"Maggie, wait. Listen, Junior came up to me after the little scene at the sculpture, and he wasn't nice, okay?" Jane looked the tall girl in the eye. "You better not tell him we had this talk either. I mean it."

But how did he know you'd be here?

Maggie nodded, her long hair swinging. She clutched her Army jacket tighter and ran out the door and down the stairs to the van. Somebody opened the door, and she climbed in. The van was already moving, still without lights, before Jane heard the clunk of the door closing. As soon as the van turned onto State College Drive, she hurried down the steps, got to Prince, and drove out.

Conversations with the Long Beach Police

She made no effort to follow the van. Instead, she drove to the Los Altos shopping center on Bellflower Boulevard, less than two miles from campus, parked, walked to the Broadway department store, and found a pay phone she hadn't used before. She dropped in a dime and called a number she knew by heart.

Fifteen minutes later, she was standing next to Prince when Terry Griswald pulled his dark green TR4 to a stop next to her. He got out and opened the passenger door. "Get in."

She shook her head. "I have to get back, but there's stuff I need to tell you."

"Captain Wingarten wants to see you."

"Terry, look–"

"Get in. There's an unmarked unit behind me. They'll take your car back to the dorm. It's important. They'll leave your keys in an envelope at the desk."

"Oh, yeah, that won't attract much attention, cops leaving me envelopes."

"Plainclothes. Nobody will know. So, c'mon, we're wasting time." And when she looked, she saw a two-year-old Ford with blackwalls and extra antennas parked one row over, engine idling. There were two people silhouetted in the front seat.

"What is this, national drive with your lights off day?"

"Huh?"

"You can just bring me back here. . ." Jane's thought for a moment. "You don't want to do that. You don't want me to drive back to the dorm by myself." He just looked at her.

She handed Terry her car keys and slid into the little sports car. He closed the door, hurried over to the Ford, and gave the keys to the driver.

Fortunately, she had an aqua scarf in her purse. She pulled it out and tied it over her hair.

To her surprise, they didn't go to the little brick police station on Second Street. Terry took Bellflower a mile north and entered a residential tract made up of small, post-war houses built when returning servicemen had eagerly been grabbing their piece of the American Dream. Despite the chill, the front door was open, but the screen door was closed. Terry tapped twice, and they went in without waiting for an answer. An older man, late fifties, maybe in his sixties, was wrapped in a dark blue blanket, sitting in the living room on a battered leather recliner with a glass of milk in his hand. A TV tray was set up next to him loaded with an empty water glass, eight or nine pill bottles, and a Swanson TV dinner displaying half a Salisbury steak submerged in clotted brown gravy. Almost all of the mashed potatoes were gone. Otherwise, the entire inventory of household furnishings seemed to consist only of a brown Naugahyde couch, a console TV, and a portable stereo sitting on a long credenza – and plants, a green jumble of spider plants hanging from the ceiling or resting in pots. A plastic mister bottle sat on the green shag carpet next to the recliner. Wingarten worked an arm out from under the blanket and gestured to the couch.

"Captain Wingarten, this is Jane, the CI I've been working with. Jane, this is my boss, Captain Wingarten."

Jane sat, smoothing her skirt over her knees. Terry leaned against the wall next to the front door. *Is he blocking the way out? I'm paranoid. You're not paranoid if they're really after you.*

She smiled.

Wingarten smiled back at her and said, "Would you like something to drink? Tab? Water?" When she shook her head, he said, "How are your classes going?"

"I have a term paper due next week and a quiz tomorrow."

"When were you going to tell us?"

Only one innocent question before the zinger. He's in a hurry.

"A week from Thursday, in the afternoon. Tell you what, Captain?"

"About Rider."

"The coxswain? Lives in the dorm? What about him? Okay, we've been on a couple of dates. He's a nice guy. I like him."

"You met him at a beach party, and there was an incident with thugs chasing you. He reported it all. Which is more than you did." Wingarten stuck his feet out from under the blanket, kicked off his moccasins, and levered up the footrest. "Forgive the informality, Miss Bailey. I have foot problems, too many years walking a beat." Terry pushed away from the wall, hurried down the hall, and returned with a small pillow and slid it under his boss's feet before pulling the blanket down and tucking it in. He did it with an easy familiarity that said he'd done it before, many times. The older man closed his eyes for a moment, sighed, and nodded thanks. "Oh, that helps. Thank you, Detective." Without being asked, Terry picked up his boss's empty water glass and took it into the kitchen. Jane heard water running. "When were you going to tell us that Rider had revealed himself as a confidential informant?" Terry set a full glass of water next to the milk on the TV tray; then he went back to leaning against the wall.

"Why do you need me if you have him? And why didn't *you* tell *me*?" Jane stopped as something dawned on her.

Wingarten drank three large gulps of milk, made a face, and said, "What we know and, for that matter, how we know it is not your concern. You *were* going to tell us, right?" He swapped glasses and drank some water.

"Sure."

"You were approached by a federal agency. Then we became your handlers, at their request."

She had an impulse to just blurt it all out, about Blank and what she suspected was the second part of her assignment. Wingarten was a police officer. He was an older man. It was hard to imagine more of an authority figure, and after all, she was barely eighteen.

Instead, she said, "Oh, good. The review before the quiz."

"Did you tell Rider of your relationship with us?"

"Yes."

"Young lady–"

Obviously, Wingarten didn't like being interrupted by a teenage girl any more than Blank. She found she didn't care. "We have something more serious. I found out tonight what BID wants to do."

They both looked at her. "I thought that might get your attention. That's why I called. They want to put something in the water, something to freak people out, and I think it's LSD. They said they need money because they want to buy a lot of it.

They had an idea to kidnap a girl from the dorm and extort money from her parents and use that money to buy the acid. But now they have–" *What exactly did Maggie say? They have money or they have the acid?* Something else clicked into place. "And Maggie Molyneaux is a chemistry major."

Wingarten started to say, "LSD in–" and then stopped himself.

Terry and Wingarten stared at each other. Wingarten drank the rest of his milk, set the glass down on the TV tray, covered his mouth with the back of his hand, and belched softly. "Excuse me, please." The two cops looked at each other again. "All right, take her back." Terry pushed away from the wall again.

Jane didn't move. Out of all the reactions she had considered, this was not one of them.

"Wait, that's it? Hey, this is important. I mean, this is what you were looking for, right?"

"We'll be in touch if we need anything more."

"Really? I don't get it."

"Just go back to class and forget all this."

After a moment, when nobody said anything, Jane stood. "Something to live for."

"Return to your normal activities. I strongly recommend that you have no further contact with any members of Burn It Down."

"That girl they were going to kidnap? It was me."

"Consider your service as a confidential informant ended, with our thanks, of course." Wingarten looked at her intently. "Ended," he repeated. "Time for you to focus on your studies. And boys." He smiled. "The life of a co-ed."

"But–"

"I doubt that there was ever a serious threat. You said yourself that these kids mostly just talk."

"My parents are old, and neither of them is in good health." *I call them my parents. My real parents are . . .* Her mind wouldn't go there. *That path leads through the corn. He's getting closer.*

"Yes, we know that, of course. Another good reason for your activities to cease. Your point?"

He picked up his water glass and a pill bottle.

"If BID or anybody else does anything to upset my parents, I, I'll do something. I'll talk. I can see the headlines: Long Beach cops force teenage girl to snitch on her classmates. Local co-ed lives in fear." In a high, quavering voice, she put both hands to her cheeks, widened her eyes, and went on. "I was *so* frightened the whole time. I just didn't know what to do. They made me spy on my friends." She batted her eyes, suddenly stopped, and leaned forward. "I promise you that, so keep it in mind when you chug your milk."

She started to leave and then turned back. "Time to cut through all this." Terry took her arm. She wished people would quit doing that. "Wait, wait a minute." She jerked her arm free. "What about Blank?"

Wingarten dropped the glass. It landed on the carpet, bounced, sprayed water, but did not break. "Who?"

"A guy named Thaddeus Blank. He came to me and said he wanted to see the reports I sent you. Kind of pudgy, in his thirties. Wears a flattop."

Wingarten stared at her. There was a drop of water on his chin. "Did you send him reports?"

"No. He's a creep; he carries a straight razor, and I think he talks to it."

Terry muttered, "You got that right. The creep part." He stepped over to Wingarten's chair, bent, and picked up the glass.

Wingarten said, "We know of Mr. Blank. It's all right."

Terry said, "When did Blank approach you?"

"A month ago after a party at the Hanging Tree."

"Where? Tree? What tree? Griswald, do you know what she's talking about?"

"Sir, it's a vacant lot next to the dorms. Kids go there to drink."

The gray-haired man had recovered. "Amazing. All right. This changes nothing. Really, just go back to school. Look for a husband. You have done very well, and we are grateful. But we'll take it from here."

"But . . ."

Terry hurried into the kitchen and brought Wingarten a new glass of water. Then he firmly took Jane's elbow and guided her to the door. When she looked back, the man in the easy chair was reading the label on one of the pill bottles. He put the bottle down and stared at her.

Griswald closed the front door and the screen. They went down the walk to his TR4, sitting at the curb, top down, sleek and cool. A minute later, as they were waiting for the light to change so they could make a right turn onto Bellflower, Terry turned to her and said, "If I ask you a question, will you answer me honestly?"

She looked straight ahead, watching an old portholed Buick lumber along in the right lane – kind of like the car her adoptive father had owned when she'd first lived with them. When it passed, Terry made the turn, and she still had not answered.

He said, "Will you?"

"Blank showed me a badge, but I don't think he's a cop."

Terry sighed, swung into the left lane and passed the Buick. "No. Not anymore."

"Just a concerned citizen helping fight the Red Menace."

"Go ahead, make fun. But that's not far from the truth. It's just his methods. Sometimes, you know, he goes too far."

"He got kicked off the force, didn't he?"

"You know how I know the Communists want to bury us? Because Khrushchev said so, that's how. And if they can't do it directly, they'll corrupt young people."

"Oh, yeah. Making little pinkos."

"The Communists are patient. They can wait, and they love young people like the ones in Burn It Down."

"What's with Wingarten? He sick?"

Terry looked at her. "Cancer. So take it easy on him, okay?"

"I'm sorry he's sick."

"Yeah. He says it really clarifies things. What about my question?"

"Depends on the question."

"Why are you doing this?"

"Doing what?"

"Quit it! Quit dancing around; this is important. Why are you acting as a confidential informant?"

"You mean being a snitch. Spying on people who think they're my friends." *Because I'm damaged and it doesn't matter.* "Seemed like a good idea at the time."

"No. You like it, Jane, I can tell, and that can get you hurt, so quit. This is not a game."

Jane grinned. "Isn't it?"

When he got to the dorm, he didn't pull up at the entrance but found a spot. A group of girls hurried up the steps, laughing as they walked quickly to beat the curfew. The radio finished something about Billy Joe and something bad that had gone down. The DJ told them not to go away because Iron Butterfly was coming up right after a word from Cal Worthington and his dog Spot. Griswald angrily snapped it off. "Hate that psychedelic shit."

Instead of reaching for the door handle or waiting for him to come around and open it, suddenly she was shivering, cold, so cold. *Because I'm damaged and it doesn't matter. And he's right. I like it.*

This is it, right? Payback. Well, I earned it. Payback is something I've known was coming ever since that night in the corn. The stalks were tall. That was it, that was the change. But I can't let what I did hurt Mildred and Raymond. I couldn't stand that. They took me in. I won't cry. I won't.

But she did.

Later, he held her and held her, and she shivered, and he talked of nothing, just words, telling her about the car and how he'd worked in a gas station to earn the money to buy it and it was the first model with windows that rolled down, how the previous year's car had side curtains that snapped in, and then they were quiet. She never answered his question. He didn't ask again.

"Jane, Wingarten meant it. You're done," he said. "We've learned what we needed to. Stay away from all of them."

When she said nothing, he turned and stared at her. She could see muscles in his jaw, clenching and unclenching. Then he climbed out of the car, walked around to her side, and jerked her door open with what she thought was something like irritation.

"Look, I know you told them I was picking you up so they could jump me in the parking lot," he said, like a man getting something off his chest. "I understand. You didn't know what they'd do."

"What? No, Terry, I didn't tell anybody." *That's why they're firing me. They think I've gone over to BID. First, Rider thinks I was spying on him at the beach party, and now Terry thinks I set him up. What else do people think they know that turns out to be wrong? What do I think I know that's wrong?*

For a moment, Terry looked as perplexed as Jane felt. He said slowly, "You're telling the truth."

"Yeah."

"Then, then I have some thinking to do."

"Terry . . ."

"Goodnight, Jane."

PROTEST!
IN ONE WEEK -- MARCH TO STOP THE WAR!
IMPEACH BOMBER JOHNSON!
ROTC OFF CAMPUS!

1968 IS THE YEAR!!!!
7:00 PM CANDLELIGHT MARCH.
THEN MEET IN FRONT OF THE BOOKSTORE.

Another copy of the flyer, complete with bright red balloon lettering, was in her mailbox. Jane shoved the flyer into her purse, and went up to her room, where she flopped on the bed and stared at the ceiling.

Deanna came in and bubbled to Jane about her date with a pitcher while she stood at the mirror and applied cold cream. Jane nodded at the right places.

That night, she had the dream again.

After dinner on Friday she was in her room, trying to learn vocabulary for next week's German quiz, when the front desk buzzed her to say she had a visitor.

Terry Griswald was waiting when she came down the stairs, leaning against the brick wall just outside the stairwell doors. He had left phone messages every day, and she had thrown them out, certain this was one more attempt to apologize, and she didn't know which she hated more – the fact that he had thought she'd set him up for the parking lot ambush or the fact that he kept saying how sorry he was, he was just upset, nothing like that had ever happened to him before. Und so weis. German quiz Monday.

She thought all this as soon as their eyes locked and she had turned to go back upstairs. He took three quick steps and caught her elbow.

"Jane, Jane, please listen." The same girl, once again working the desk, goggled at them then went back to Jacqueline Suzanne.

"Terry, quit, okay? It happened, and it's done, and I'm dating a really nice guy. Please, quit doing this. But listen, thanks for letting me cry on your shoulder."

For a moment, he looked confused. Then he rolled his eyes and muttered something about girls that she didn't catch.

"Jane, it's not about us."

He looked around. On the TV in the common area, Captain Kirk kissed a green girl, and three boys yelled, "Work out!"

Terry leaned in and whispered, "Jane, we need to talk."

"That's my line, except we have talked."

He blurted out, "Have you heard from any of the BID people?"

"No."

"Why haven't you filed any reports? It's been days."

"A – Wingarten told me I was done. B – so did you." She looked into his eyes. "Talk to Rider. And . . ." She paused, the whole backstory suddenly clear to her. "Oh man, now I get it. You 'fired' me assuming that I'd go on, on my own, and if something went wrong, you could say, 'Oh, it's not our fault. We told her to quit.' Very clever."

Griswald had the decency to blush. "I didn't know about it until Wingarten told me. He said it was for your own good, to protect you."

"You guys are something else."

"It's war, Jane. Really."

Now she knew something was wrong. She jabbed at him, putting a little heat on her words. "Tell me." Terry licked his lips and looked around again. "All right," Jane said. "Let's walk. But I swear if somebody tries to drag you into a car, I'm going to let them."

He managed a grin.

Terry had the top up on the TR4. They sat inside. Jane twisted around awkwardly in the bucket seat to face him. He licked his lips again. "Okay, Rider was a good CI. He kept his eyes open even when it looked like nothing was going on. Now we can't get in touch with him."

"The crew team is at the second San Diego Regatta," she said. "I have a number where they're staying."

But he didn't call last night to tell me how they'd been seeded and if the lead stroke was over the flu.

"Well, that's a relief," Terry said. "Give it to me, and I'll call."

He was talking to an empty seat. " Jane, wait–"

But she was gone. Running.

She had to go upstairs to find the number in her purse, and when she got back to the phone in the lobby, naturally, Terry was standing next to it, a handful of dimes and quarters spread on the shelf. After giving the operator the number and depositing seventy-five cents for the first three minutes, at last she heard the hotel operator. "Room number, please?"

"Uh, I'm not sure. His name's Rider, and he's with the Long Beach crew team."

"One moment, please."

The phone rang half a dozen times, and just as the hotel operator broke in to say, "Your party is not answering," somebody shouted, "Hello, Long Beach Oar House." In the background loud music and voices almost drowned out the speaker.

"This is–"

The Bell operator came on with "Please deposit fifty cents for an additional three minutes."

She jammed in two of Griswald's quarters. "This is Jane. Is Rider there?"

There was a pause, a hesitation. "Uh, Jane? Yeah, this is Clark. Hey, Rider's not here right now. Want me to have him call you?"

"Yes! But he's with you guys in San Diego, right?"

"Well, sure. Where else would he be? We got a race in the morning, and if – when – we win" – loud shouts drowned him out for a moment, "Win!" "Yeah!" "Kick butt! Go 49er's!" And so on – "we'll race the semis in the afternoon. Why, Jane? You checking up on our cox?"

"No, no, I just hadn't heard from him, you know, and I worried a little. He's out, huh?"

"Uh, yeah, you know, see the sights. You want him to call?"

"Of course I do, but it's not necessary. I have a German test next week, so I'll talk to him after the races."

"Got it."

"Who do you race tomorrow?"

"Orange Coast."

"Rider's got a date, doesn't he?" *Useless questions and then a zinger.*

"Some girl from Shell and Oar," he said and then added, "Shit!"

"All right, you guys win, okay?"

"Please deposit fifty–" She hung up.

"He's fine," she said. Terry nodded.

The crew team came back Sunday night, but it must have been late, because Rider didn't call. They missed each other at breakfast in the cafeteria on Monday and then were submerged in quizzes, term papers, and school.

Andromeda

For just a moment, Andromeda considered the LSD tab – a postage-stamp-size piece of paper with Minnie Mouse flipping the bird printed on it and loaded with a drop of mighty fine acid – before slipping it into a cup of lukewarm coffee and stirring quickly with her index finger. She scooped the soggy paper out, sucked it off the end of her finger, chewed, and swallowed. *Waste not want not.* Her grandma used to say that after grandpa had bitten the tuna with his second stroke and the old bag had come to live with them. "Learn to cook. You're not pretty, but a good cook can always find a husband." *Thanks a lot, Granny.*

The big girl was in the cafeteria, standing outside the double doors to the kitchen, next to the urns of coffee and wheeled shelves where students were supposed to bus their trays. She was wearing the paper hat and apron of a cafeteria worker, and in fact, she did have a job bussing tables and cleaning the Bunn-O-Matic coffee machines – just next door in the Greek section, not here in the dorm section. But nobody looked closely. *There she is, sitting by the doors with other princesses. This is kind of mean, but, but . . . nobody ever showed her a magazine ad that said, "Catch a boy with Wonder Bread."* She put the loaded coffee cup on a saucer, set them on the cart she would use to clear tables, and rolled down the aisle. Deanna was distracted, talking to some other establishment princess about useless middle-class shit and didn't see what Andromeda did as she collected dishes from tables and switched the loaded coffee cup for Deanna's.

Wait, wasn't it supposed to be half a tab? When she had slipped it in the cup, it had looked like it was whole. *Aw, no, it couldn't have been.*

Junior hid his drugs inside a stuffed armadillo they'd brought home from a very loaded trip to Tijuana that had included getting their picture taken in a cart being pulled by an unfortunate donkey painted to look like a zebra. She had slid a finger into the slit in the armadillo's stomach and found a bunch of tabs just like she'd been told she would. Junior always had the best shit. She'd pulled out the half-tab Junior had had ready and then swiped an extra one for her own use. That was all she had, so of course, it was the half-tab that she'd given the princess in the pukey orange tent dress. Andromeda's mother had bought her one like it the last time she'd gone home. Back at school, she'd traded the dress for a lid of what Pryboy the dealer had claimed was Acapulco Gold.

Andromeda watched as Deanna took a sip. Dorm coffee was so bad that she didn't seem to notice anything when she turned back and sipped again. To Andromeda's surprise, she finished the whole cup, taking in the entire dose, so Andromeda snickered and quickly ducked back into the kitchen just as Jane walked into the cafeteria and sat down next to her friend. *The new girl, Jane, doesn't really fit with the rest of us. I hope Junior doesn't keep her. He hasn't given her a family name yet, and that's a good sign. Junior knows everything. He's so smart, and he loves me, and he always has really good shit.* The name tag pinned to Andromeda's cafeteria-worker vest had her birth name, but that felt like something she'd shed, an old self. *Do armadillos shed their skins?* She giggled. Waste not want not was kicking in. She giggled again. She was Andromeda. She was part of the family, a family that didn't care how often she washed her hair or if she could cook, and who loved her more than her parents or anybody else.

Now the three princesses were talking. Suddenly Deanna started laughing and waving her arms, reaching out to touch Jane's cheek. Then she jumped to her feet, knocked her chair over, and ran to the double doors, bouncing off and then pushing one open and laughing, still laughing. New-girl Jane was up before the doors could swing shut, running after her friend.

Andromeda hustled over with a tray, started clearing the table, and replaced Deanna's cup. Junior was so smart. He knew the pigs would suspect drugs and check everything Deanna had eaten or drunk. Now the cup they found would be clean. Junior was so smart. Andromeda almost regretted stealing the extra tab, now safely hidden in her wallet behind a real postage stamp, from his stash in Angie the Armadillo, but her last trip had been so mind-blowing that she hadn't been able to resist. Thinking about the tab made her feel good. She would take it, maybe just half, and then go to her three o'clock lecture, sit in the back, and groove on the slides and the brilliant colors. She decided to go in the bathroom and do half now and then walk up the hill to class.

But when she was locked in a stall, sitting on the toilet seat, the space behind the real postage stamp was empty. Andromeda's first thought was that now she'd have to go to class straight, which was always a bummer, but then she thought: *Where did it go? I had a half-tab for the princess and a whole one for me, and now there's nothing. Did they stick together? Did I give her* all *of it? A tab and a half?* Her close-set eyes squinted shut as she tried to think. Maybe she shouldn't have smoked that joint before getting the shit out of Angie. She searched her entire purse again, just to be sure, and then walked out of the bathroom, trying to look casual, to *maintain,* but feeling the acid kick in – just the little bit she'd taken -- trying not to giggle at how funny the kids looked with colors sprouting out of their mouths. *That's powerful shit. Oh, yeah.* Outside the kitchen, she was sure that all the straights were looking at her. She fumbled with her hat, put her name tag back on the rack – it took three tries, but nobody was paying attention – and hurried up the hill. *Now I won't have to go to class straight.*

This is a Test

Outside on the lawn, the small girl in the orange dress was trying to walk up into the sky. She had kicked off her white flats and, holding her arms out to her sides, was walking up a set of stairs that only she could see, placing one stockinged foot in front of the other, looking up and smiling, smiling and laughing. The crowd of kids around her watched, amazed, and Jane could hear people say things like, "Must be some good shit."

Jane caught her friend's arm. Deanna turned to face her, smiling. "You are so beautiful," she said. She touched Jane's cheek and laughed. "Beautiful."

"Take it easy, Deanna. I'm right here." Jane had read lurid accounts of people dropping acid, and there were kids in the dorm who claimed to have tripped, but this was her first direct experience, and she was scared, scared and confused. Her roommate a head? Impossible, except that now she was just staring at a spot over Jane's left shoulder, staring and frowning.

All at once, something clicked in Jane's head, and she wasn't scared anymore. Oh, the fear was still there, she could feel it in a corner of her head, but it was like when she was being chased in the corn and, all at once, she knew to run to the old well, and she was still scared, sure she was, but it was like when daddy was working on his books and had the radio on low, background noise. Deanna was tripping. She wasn't a doper. Therefore, somebody had slipped her the acid. But that didn't matter now. What mattered was getting care for her roommate, the girl who'd shown her around campus and who'd helped her not be lonely in the dorm. Her friend. Finding whoever had done this to Deanna would come later.

"When you talk, I can *see* it, see the colors of what you're saying. It's beautiful. You're beautiful."

Jane looked at the nearest kid, a pledge in a TKE t-shirt, and yelled, "Call an ambulance! Now! Run!" He ran.

Jane held Deanna as she began to shake and froth appeared at the corners of her mouth. Her eyes rolled back, and she sank to the ground, moaning, laughing, and muttering incomprehensible things. Jane sat next to her roommate and cradled her in her arms until the ambulance wheeled in and stopped, lights flashing. While the white-suited men checked Deanna's pulse, thumbed back her eyelids to peer in her eyes, and took her blood pressure, Jane ran back into the cafeteria and grabbed Deanna's purse from where it had been hanging on the back of her chair. She'd get the books later. She gave the purse to one of the men in white and watched as they loaded her friend on a stretcher and slid her into the ambulance. The last Jane saw of Deanna, she was motionless, eyes wide and staring. Jane told herself that was better than just the whites showing. One of the men gently wiped the froth from Deanna's cheek before the doors closed, and then the ambulance drove across the grass to West Campus Drive. They turned on the siren at once.

Jane got Deanna's books, stacked them with hers, and ran all the way back to the dorm.

In her room, she pulled the box out from under her bed and grabbed the piece of paper with the phone number she'd hoped never to use. She thought about the call, one she had hoped never to make, and then decided that she had to. She drove to the shopping center and called and left a message. Then she called Terry Griswald from a different pay phone. She got his Ansafone.

Conversations with Friends and Others

"Okay, this is . . . you know who it is. I know this is your apartment, and I'm glad you have an answering machine. Terry, listen, today at school, my roommate Deanna freaked out. Right in front of the cafeteria. It was pretty bad. I was there, and I saw it, and an ambulance came, and I think they took her to Long Beach Memorial. Acid. The ambulance driver said it looked like an acid trip. I wanted you to know."

She knew Rider had crew practice in the afternoon, so she cut poli sci and drove Prince to the boathouse at Marine Stadium. Practice was over, and he was directing the clean-up, watching the teams hose salt water off the sixty-foot-long, razor-slim eight-man shell as it rested on wooden and canvas racks. He looked up when one of the tall rowers nudged him. For a moment, he just looked surprised. Then he grinned. Knowing the propensity of the team to use hoses indiscriminately, Jane stayed back and waved. He said something to the kid with the hose and trotted over to her. He reached out to embrace her. She stepped back.

"You're all wet."

"Oh, yeah. We had some coxswain-tossing after practice." When she looked blank, he added, "It's a tradition to throw the cox in after you win a race. Sometimes, if I've worked them a little too hard, they do it just for fun."

"Too many Big Tens?" He nodded. "They throw you in the water?"

"Well, first they have to catch you. My guys beat the varsity for distance this time. I really flew."

"How was the regatta?"

"Uh, good, good. UCLA beat us in the semis. Jane, what are you doing here?"

"Rider, are you still sending in reports?"

At that, he took her elbow and moved away from the boats. "No. They told me to quit. I may have to get a job, and if I do, I don't think I can be a cox anymore. Why?"

"Deanna freaked out. Rider, I think somebody slipped her acid. She was climbing stairs that weren't there. Talking about seeing colors. They took her to Memorial."

As she said it, she felt the beginning of tears. She fought them back. "Uh, Jane, does Deanna, I mean, I don't know her very well and–"

"No! She doesn't smoke grass or anything."

"I had to ask. You think this is what BID had in mind?"

She shook her head and swiped some moisture from her cheek. "No, not exactly. I think this was a test."

Behind them, the varsity shell came in to the dock. The coxswain jumped out and held the boat steady while the tall crewmen carefully climbed out.

"You called Griswald?"

"I left a message. I feel like we should do something, but I don't know what."

"Whoa, Jane, if somebody–"

"BID. It was them."

"–slipped her acid, this is getting scary. You say you told Griswald?"

"Yeah."

"Good. I think you're right about BID." He grinned. "It's time for me to have a serious talk with Junior."

Behind them, the coxswain called directions as the varsity lifted their boat out of the water and walked it to the racks preparatory to hosing it off. Rider's team was lined up next to their boat, looking at him expectantly.

"Rider, no."

"I'm not scared of him."

"Blank's in this somehow, I know he is."

"Wait a minute." He trotted over to his boat. "Okay, hands on." The team gripped the sides of the boat. "Roll it to your waist." They lifted the fragile shell off the rack, turning it hull up. Water drained out. "To your shoulders. Now walk it forward." A moment later, the boat was stowed, and the team was heading for the showers.

Rider trotted back over to Jane. "Okay. I still think Junior will have a lot to say once he's encouraged."

"Blank calls me or I have a number – he wrote it on my arm that night in the field – where I can leave a message. And one of the girls who works the desk said I had a call from some guy who wouldn't leave a message. I thought it was Griswald, but now I'm not so sure."

Rider said, "When did this happen?"

"The message was yesterday. And I've been in class all morning, and then Deanna freaked out, and I came out here to see you."

They agreed Rider would go back to the dorm after he showered and that if Griswald called either of them, they would tell him about Deanna and the acid. If Blank called, Jane said she would try to set up a meeting.

Neither happened. Jane visited Deanna at Long Beach Memorial and brought her textbooks. Jane thought her roommate looked pale and tired as she lay against the sheets. And scared.

The next afternoon, Jane took up a position on the lawn across from *Anonymous*, where Junior sat with three of the girls – not, she noticed, Maggie Molyneaux. Their heads were together in intense conversation. She pretended to read the massive *English Literature to 1500* text she had lugged up the hill before deciding to cut class.

Jane watched for a while, waiting for inspiration to strike. She could go up to the group and act friendly, or she could confront them about the acid. Neither option seemed like it would be productive.

Then Junior and two of the girls got to their feet and trudged down the hill toward the cafeteria. Nowhere Girl was left sitting by herself, smoking a cigarette and picking at her nail polish. Jane collected her books and joined her, dropping English Literature on the grass and sitting on it, carefully tucking her skirt around her knees. "Hi." *What's her name? I can't call her Nowhere Girl to her face.* "What's happening?" The other girl looked up. "You just missed Junior. He went down to the cafeteria with the other girls, but you can catch them 'cause they just left. They're gonna get some coffee and then junior's gonna split. He's got an important meeting."

"Nah. I'll just hang here with you for a while." Nowhere Girl either nodded or her head drooped, exhausted from the intensity of the conversation. "Hey, I'm undeclared, just can't decide on a major." More silence. *Maybe she's unconscious.* "Hey, this is the part where you say something." Another blank look. "What's your major?"

That got a brief look up and a small smile. "Psychology maybe." Another shrug. "I haven't decided yet."

"Cool. I'm thinking about psych or maybe sociology, you know, helping people. So, how did you meet Junior?"

Now Nowhere Girl looked up and offered a real smile. *Tranquility, that's it. Her stupid family name is Tranquility.*

"Last year, I was just sitting on this bench by the stairs on the end of Liberal Arts One, you know, and I was really bummed out because all my classes sucked and I didn't know anybody and I'd just had this huge fight with my mom about this stupid guy she was seeing, and Junior came up, and he sat down, and he just started talking to me. And I felt better, way better like, like–"

"Like you had somebody who was listening, really listening."

All at once, the vacant look was completely gone, and Jane saw a real person, a girl who left home for college because it had to be better, couldn't be worse. And at last she had friends, and if they did bad things, got her to do bad things, well, gas, grass, or ass – nobody rides for free, right?

"What's your name? Your real name?"

Tranquility just shook her head. Then she looked over her shoulder before blurting out, "And he has plans, big plans. Did you hear about General LeMay?" She was really looking at Jane now, her face alight.

"Uh, no, not really."

"Do you even know who he is?" Before Jane could answer, Tranquility rushed on. "He's George Wallace's running mate, and he says it's cool to use nuclear weapons. He says the world wouldn't end, but we know better, and we have to stop shit like that."

"Wow."

"No shit, Jane. Heavy stuff. Like those Negroes at the Olympics giving the black power salute. Important stuff."

"Junior talks about this?"

"All kinds of important stuff. He's so smart. We have to wake up the pro . . . uh . . ."

"Proletariat."

"Yeah! That's it."

"And he listens to you."

"Yeah, yeah, that's it, and he knows stuff, and he's so smart, and he loves all of us."

"You guys are a pretty tight group."

"We're a family."

"Wow. Really, that's so cool." Inspiration struck. "Good talking to you, Tranquility. If the others come back, tell 'em I said hi." She collected her purse and book and hurried down the hill to the dorm parking lot, where she dumped everything in Prince's back seat and drove across the street to student parking. Junior had once told her that he hated getting up early and only took afternoon classes, and that meant his VW van would be parked at the back of the enormous lot, close to Atherton Avenue. She knew what it looked like, and she had memorized the license number, so she cruised up one quarter-mile row and down another.

She didn't find the rusty van, but luck was with her. Out of the corner of her eye, she caught a glimpse of Mutton Chop himself in a field jacket, walking slowly along the row ahead of her. She immediately stopped and watched. Junior wouldn't suspect anything; people stopped and waited for cars to leave a parking spot all the time. But where were the girls? He shouldn't have suspected, but for some reason, he stopped and looked around. Then he turned and walked toward her.

He's seen me.

But Junior looked right to left and then walked quickly between cars to the next row over. He couldn't find his car.

Jane slammed Prince into reverse and backed up, keeping ahead of him. He stopped for a moment and actually scratched his head in a parody of "Now, where did I leave it?" The he suddenly walked briskly between two almost-identical red VW Beetles to the next row. Now Jane could see the top of the van. One more row, and she would have found it, but this was even better. She heard it start up. It backed out and headed for the exit.

I've never tried to follow another car before, but how hard can it be? She made sure to keep at least two cars between them as they turned out onto Bellflower Boulevard and then south to Second Street. It looked like Junior was heading for downtown Long Beach, maybe to the Pike for a beer or a tattoo.

Jane followed to Ocean Boulevard, glad that Junior never once looked around. Suddenly, at the corner of Ocean Boulevard and Shoreline Drive, the van swerved into the left-turn lane and sped down a side street between a circular skyscraper and an old building with a green tile roof. Jane had moved one lane over to keep a truck between her car and her quarry, and she blew past the street/alley. She turned right at the next light, hung an illegal U-turn in the middle of the block, and got back onto Ocean Boulevard. On Prince's radio, Jim Morrison told her this was the end, and it looked like he was right. She turned down the street Junior had taken, drove slowly past the entrance to underground parking, and drove around, scanning the Long Beach Arena parking lot, trying to look in all directions at once, but she saw no rusty VW van. She got a ticket from the guard and drove into the enormous parking lot, cruising for a while, but after half an hour of fruitless searching, she gave up, paid to get out of the parking lot, and went back to the dorm.

"Okay, Blank contacts you, right?"

It was in the afternoon the day after Jane's fruitless attempt to follow Junior.

Rider and Jane were in the Cerritos common area, where they could sit in the worn, comfortable chairs and compare notes. She told him about her attempt to follow Junior and how she had lost him.

"He calls me and then comes by and picks me up in this big Caddy."

"Well, I don't like it, but I guess we just wait. Sooner or later–"

"I've still got the number he wrote on my arm. Let's call again." Jane rummaged in her purse and pulled out a scrap of paper. They hurried to the phone and waited while a girl finished her call – asking Dad to send a few bucks because her books had cost more than she thought – and then Jane dropped in coins and dialed the number.

After four rings, she heard, "Acapulco Inn."

Bar? Hotel? Bar. Like before, talking in the background.

"Is there a man there named Blank?"

There was a pause. "Blank?"

"Right. That's his last name. He's in his forties, I think, and–"

"Yeah, yeah. Okay, whadda ya wanna tell him?"

"Ask him to call Jane. He's got the number."

"Hey, honey, whyn't you come down here and hang out? He'll show up."

"Oh, far out. Groovy."

"Yeah, baby, come on down. I'm Ray. I'll save you a seat at the bar."

"Something to live for."

"What?"

Jane sighed. "Thanks, Ray. Sounds groovy. Just give Mr. Blank the message." They sat for a while and then Rider left do homework.

When Jane went back to her room, Deanna was there, lying on her back with an arm thrown over her eyes.

"Deanna, hey, they let you out. How are you feeling?"

Without moving her arm, the tiny girl said, "Ever had a stomach pump?"

"Ewww."

"Yeah, tell me about it. But I feel all right, except–"

"What?"

"The doctor said I ingested a lot of acid. I might have" – she moved her arm and swallowed convulsively, and Jane could see that her eyes were red-rimmed and swollen – "you know, f-fl-flashbacks. Maybe for a year. Oh God! Can you, can you see me in front of a class of sixth graders, and all at once I'm going, 'Hey, kids, look at the snakes?'"

"Did you see snakes?"

"No. I'm serious, Jane. I'm trying to talk to you here."

"Shove over." Jane sat on foot of the bed. "I talked to a doctor at the hospital. He said you had a good trip because you're basically a happy person and you were happy when the acid hit you. Flashbacks – and they may not happen – will probably not be too bad."

Deanna wiped her nose, clutched the tissue. "Not snakes?"

Jane grinned. "Well, friendly ones. Fuzzy." They both laughed, and for a moment, Jane thought it would be all right.

Suddenly the small girl was crying, not wailing, not sobbing, just sitting on the bed, clutching a pillow to her chest, with tears leaking out of her eyes and running down the sides of her face before trickling onto her blouse, the good one with the wide neck and blue-and-white horizontal stripes. Jane stood up, grabbed a handful of tissues, and sat down next to her. She gave her the tissues and held her hand.

Between sobs, Deanna said, "And now I've got a police record. They, they wanted to know where I got the acid. I told them I didn't get it anywhere, that I don't even know anybody who does drugs, but they didn't believe me, you know, they didn't believe me, and nobody's ever thought I was l–lying before. I tell the truth, really. Then another policeman, young, with black hair and a crewcut, he came in and talked to the men interviewing me." Her eyes widened. "Plainclothes. I've seen him before! He picked you up in that little sports car." Jane nodded. "Anyway, he took the police out into the hall, and when they came back, they seemed to believe my story. Did you do that?"

Jane shook her head.

After Deanna repaired her makeup, they met Rider and walked up the hill for a quick dinner of lettuce with Thousand Island, followed by green beans, macaroni and cheese, and a chocolate chip cookie. Then they came back and, when Jane found no messages in her mailbox, settled in to wait. Jane was worried about how to get rid of Deanna, but Deanna looked at the two of them, pleaded a sample lesson plan due tomorrow, and went upstairs. Jane said if Blank hadn't called by ten pm, when guests had to leave the lobby, they'd give up for the night. "We'll set up a meeting, and then, when he drops me off, we'll follow him in your car."

Rider said, "Tell me again why we're doing this."

"Blank's involved somehow. And he's a bad guy. I mean, he talks to his razor! And he's all we've got. Those guys on the beach, I've been thinking about them, and what if they were Blank's stooges, the ones I met out in the field? Except for the hair, they were sort of familiar, and they could have been wearing wigs."

"I guess," Rider said doubtfully. "I know two guys with long hair who wear short wigs when they go to National Guard meetings. I guess it could work the other way."

But nothing happened that night.

The next day was the demonstration.

After lunch, Rider and Jane were sitting on a couch in the Cerritos TV room. Blank had not answered the message Jane had left last night, they'd been unable to find any of the BID members on campus, and they were out of ideas.

The news was on. It showed men in jackets like Maggie and Junior wore, but these carried rifles and jumped out of helicopters into a jungle. Rider couldn't take his eyes off the screen.

Jane happened to look out the glass doors and saw the black Caddy as it bounced up the drive and into the lot.

"Rider, quick, Blank's not gonna call because he's here now. Quick, go out the other door and get your car. I'll stall, and we'll follow him when he leaves."

"Got it." He sprinted out the doors on the opposite side of the lobby.

Jane counted to twenty and then walked toward the front desk. She heard the phone ring and slowed. The girl on the switchboard, a red-headed freshman Jane had met once, waved and said, "Jane, Jane, you got a call." She pointed to the phone on the wall next to the stairs.

Then she covered the mouthpiece and, eyes wide, whispered, "Mobile operator."

"Parking lot. Now." It was Blank, of course.

The tall skinny guy got out from the front and held the rear door for her. She got in next to Blank. The skinny guy didn't get back behind the wheel; instead, he closed the door behind her and leaned against it, arms crossed.

"What was so urgent?"

Watching his face carefully, she said, "My roommate, Deanna, flipped out, probably on LSD, and she's not a doper, so somebody slipped it to her. They took her to Long Beach Memorial, but she's out now."

Watching his face did no good. Expressionless, Blank sat for a moment, just looking at her. The sides of his flattop shone with oil, and the front stood up in short spikes. He was dressed in a gray suit, white shirt, and narrow black tie, a silver tie clip with some kind of stone, maybe a cat's eye, set in the middle, his snap-brim hat on the package shelf behind them. When he twisted sideways to face her, she could see the edge of a black leather strap under his right armpit. She'd seen that kind of strap before, on the quiet men who had moved her to what they called a safe house even though sometimes it was just an apartment. She realized that he'd asked her something and she hadn't been paying attention, lost for a moment in thoughts of always learning a new name and never going outside except with an adult. And corn fields. And a bad man chasing her. *And the corn rustled. I couldn't feel a breeze, but it rustled. As if it knew I was there.*

Blank just looked at her.

Jane said, "You knew."

"We saw the report. Yes, of course, we knew."

"I'm sorry, what did you say before?"

"I asked about the child involved. I hope you pay better attention in class. It's im–"

"Her name is Deanna Mecum, and she's my friend, and she's not a child."

"Don't interrupt and don't contradict me. And you think this girl was turned on, stoned, probably toked up on some reefer, and then took, I mean dropped, LSD?"

"No! If you mean she took the drug on purpose, no, absolutely not. Deanna wouldn't. She's going to be a teacher, but if this goes on her record, there's no chance."

"But she was on drugs."

"Yeah, lying on the grass, staring at the sky, waving her arms. Her dress was ruined."

"Yes, acid, definitely LSD. She was tripping. Okey-doke, I knew it, yes, I knew this would happen. Okey-doke. Now we know."

"The cops are trying to figure out where she got the acid. I assume you are too. What do you need me to do?"

"What? Figure out where she got it? Her pusher, of course."

Jane shook her head. "Someone slipped it to her. What do you want me to do?"

"You? Oh my, nothing, nothing at all.

"What about BID?"

"Oh, I wouldn't worry about them. We'll keep an eye on them, but I think, like you said, they're mostly talk."

Jane stared at him for a moment. Then she shook her head. "You mean I'm done?"

"We have what we need, so yes, with our thanks, you are free to return to classes and sock hops and the life of a college co-ed."

Sock hops? "But–"

He reached across Jane and tapped on the window. The tall guy opened the door and the dome light reflected off Blank's slick black hair. He stared at her and smiled, and when she didn't move quickly enough, he made a shooing gesture with both hands.

She got out. The Cadillac rolled silently out of the parking lot and disappeared around the corner. A moment later, Rider slid to a stop in his Falcon, and she jumped in.

"Blank says I'm done."

"Wow, everybody's firing us." He tried to grin. "If we were smart, we'd listen." But as he said it, he dropped the Falcon into first, popped the clutch, and the chase was on.

Except it wasn't much of a chase. The large black car was easy to follow as it took Pacific Coast Highway south and then turned on Second Street toward downtown Long Beach. Even the notorious lights on Second Street were not a huge problem. They were separated a few times but always found Blank's car at the next light. Livingston turned into Ocean Boulevard, and then the harbor was on their left, with tankers and car carrier ships at anchor.

The Caddy turned next to a tall, circular building. Rider had no choice but to drive by. By the time he turned around and came back, the car was gone.

"That's where Junior went," Jane said. Rider nodded and followed. They turned into the lot, drove around for a few minutes, then parked and got out.

"Rainbow Pier," he said as they stood and he pointed to the structure across the water. "The guys come here every now and then. They always dare me to get a tattoo."

"So, what tattoo do they want you to get?"

"A little Mickey Mouse saying, 'I'm drunk.'"

"Yeah, who wouldn't want something that bitchin'?"

Jane thought that their careers as detectives were pitiful.

"Let's hang out for a while, see if he comes back."

Blank Three

The reason Jane and Rider couldn't find Blank's Caddy was because it was in the parking beneath the International Tower. The apartment associated with the parking was on the twentieth floor, with one wall of floor-to-ceiling glass that looked out over the harbor, Catalina, and, on the right, parts of Long Beach. There was a balcony off the living room, and if Blank had been on the balcony with binoculars, he could have spotted Jane and Rider standing next to Rider's Falcon, but he was otherwise occupied and he never went out on the balcony when the sun was out. Soon, after it was dark, Blank would be able to step outside, but not now, no, not during the day when they might see. Blank was sitting on a white Naugahyde couch, dressed in what he considered his uniform – white shirt and dark tie. His coat was carefully hung in the master bedroom closet with precisely enough space on each side to prevent the collar from being crushed. His other uniform, the one with the medals, the one he'd be able to wear soon, was laid out on the bed.

Junior Higgins stood in front of him. He looked terrified. *Good, he should be.*

"Are you going to kill me?"

"Oh no, no. Not unless you make another mistake." Blank continued cleaning his straight razor. Stroking Miss Telstar sometimes soothed him, but not now. *This hippie has jeopardized everything. It's the drugs, of course. I should have known better than to trust a dope fiend.*

Junior was standing in front of him, hands shoved deep into the pockets of his dirty field jacket. He could not take his eyes off the razor. When Blank and his driver had walked into the apartment, Junior had already been there, surrounded by silent men who stood waiting, as ordered. They knew how to do as they were told. *The hippie doesn't yet. I believe he can be taught. For his sake, I hope so, but sometimes I am too soft.*

"I was doing what you told me to," Junior – *what a ridiculous name* – whined.

"Stop that this instant." Blank sighed, folded Miss Telstar, and slipped her into his pants pocket. "Our enemies do not make mistakes. Okey-doke, please tell me what you thought you were supposed to do."

When Junior didn't answer immediately, Blank's hand strayed toward his pocket. Junior paled and started talking. *Good.*

"Scare one of them, scare one of Jane's friends."

"Why?"

"You want Jane to report dangerous radical activity on campus, and if she can't find it, we'll show it to her. That's what you said."

"Did I say I wanted the girl hospitalized? Serious police involvement?"

"Uh – "

"I did not." Blank sighed. "Now the police believe the child was fed the drug, not that she took it willingly. Okey-doke. Why did I say I wanted Jane to make such a report?"

"Why? Uh, oh yeah, you want this, this, like a big event, like a demonstration, like tonight, so you can come in and, and – I don't know, I'm sorry, I'm sorry."

"You don't know because I haven't told you." Gently. The kid relaxed a little. *Good.*

"Oh right, right, yeah. Yes, sir. You haven't told me. That part of the plan is, like, secret."

Despite feeling a little better, Junior couldn't stop licking his lips. Sweat ran down his face, into his black mutton chop sideburns.

I made sure he watched while I corrected one of my soldiers last week. I assumed that would make him careful, but obviously, I was wrong. Soft. I'm just too soft.

Blank leaned forward and stared at Junior. "And how were you to do this?"

Lick, lick. Convulsive swallow. "Acid. I was gonna put a little acid in one of her friend's drinks, like, freak her out."

"And did you do that? Wait, first, where did you get the LSD?"

"From you. You gave it to me." Junior's eyes darted toward the second bedroom.

I need to move the setup. To the warehouse, I suppose.

Blank made an impatient "come on" gesture.

"Put it in her coffee or something."

"Okey-doke. That's right. But that's not what you did, is it?" Junior's eyes rolled, and Blank thought the hippie might faint, and he didn't want that, not yet. He said gently, "It's all right, you can tell me." Blank kept his hands still, but it was not easy. Miss Telstar was so close. His voice was soft, almost comforting. "What did you really do?"

Junior couldn't meet his eyes. He licked his lips and mumbled, "Andromeda."

"Andromeda." *Another silly name.* "Yes. One of your girls."

"She works in the cafeteria, and it would be easy for her, see, because she has the hat and the, the name badge."

"Easy. It would be easy for her." Blank's voice was so soft Junior had to strain to hear it. "But she didn't do it, did she?"

"That's it! She didn't. It's her fault! She gave the girl too much. See, she stole a tab from me. I told her to take half a tab and put it in the girl's – Deanna's – in her coffee, only she took a tab and a half out of the armadillo, and Andromeda, she took the extra tab for herself, and she messed up, and it all got in the coffee, and it's her fault not mine. She did it. She's a head, and she fucks up all the time."

Armadillo? Is he farther gone than I thought? Blank frowned at the profanity. Junior blanched. Blank's hands did not move. "I see. So I should discipline her, not you."

"Yes! Yes! She did it."

"All right. Now I understand. You may go now."

"Thank you, sir, oh, thank you." Junior sagged again, this time with relief. One of Blank's men caught him by his wide leather belt and held him up. Junior pushed his hair back and nodded.

Junior's hands were shaking so badly that he shoved them back into his pockets as he started to say something else, but suddenly there were Blank's guys between him and the door, three of them now, all wearing suits minus the wigs they used when pretending to be hippies.

"Oh," Blank said. "There is one more thing."

"No, no, please." Junior made a break for the door but was intercepted.

He ran for the bathroom.

Blocked again.

Then the door. Tripped, he went to his knees. He got up, backed away.

Blank enjoyed watching as much as the ex-cops enjoyed chasing. Unfortunately, Junior was not very quick, and they only got to play with him a little before the tallest one snagged Junior's collar. Then they had him, and it was Blank's turn. He stood up, straightened his tie, patted his pocket, not to make sure Miss Telstar was in there – he always knew where she was – but just because it felt good.

"Hold him."

Junior was blubbering now, tears and mucus running down his face and into his moustache, and twisting to get out of the grip of the men who held his arms, but it was useless – they'd had a lot of practice. Blank stood and looked at him kindly. "Let's take our young friend into the kitchen, please."

The men dragged Junior into the kitchen and held him against the turquoise counter.

"Are you right-handed?"

"What, what?"

"That's okay," Blank said, soothing now. "It's all right now, don't you worry. Okey-doke, I'll choose for you."

"Yes! Right-handed! I'm right-handed. Please, no, it won't happen again."

"There, there. Now you understand that I must know that my orders are carried out exactly as I say. You understand. Exactly."

"Yes!"

"Tell me what I said, please."

"Exactly! Do what you say exactly."

Miss Telstar appeared in Blank's left hand. Sharpening her hadn't soothed him, but this would. This sort of thing *always* did. He flicked her open, admiring how her blade reflected the fluorescent lights. For a moment, he amused himself by moving the spot of reflected light across Junior's face and watching the hippie flinch. Then he walked around behind the hippie and began crooning:

"Ooh the shark bites,

has such teeth, dear,

and he shows them

pearly white."

Blank shuffled around the kitchen, crooning his tune and doing his dance, sink to refrigerator to stove and back again. The men who held Junior did not seem to think this was odd, but Junior's eyes bugged out, and his teeth actually began to chatter.

"What? What?" Junior's eyes rolled wildly as Blank stopped in front of him and moved the reflection across his face again.

"Just a jackknife, hmm, hmm, hmmm. Pull up his left sleeve. Tidy. We must be tidy. Hold his left arm out over the sink."

"No! No! Please!"

"Not the left? You prefer the right?"

Junior could only stare. Blank began singing again. "Pearly white, oh yes." Suddenly he stopped. "What happened on October 4, 1957?"

"What? I don't know! I'm sorry! I'll learn! I'll learn what happened. I'll do anything you want." Tears streamed down Junior's face.

"Of course you will. Okey-doke."

Manny and his pal held Junior, and after looking at Blank, who nodded to the left, they pulled the left sleeve of his jacket up past the elbow. They moved his arm over the sink.

Blank looked thoughtfully at Junior's forearm, admiring the network of blue veins that ran down to his wrist. Then he drew a line from elbow to wrist with the blade of his razor, gently, not breaking the skin. Junior sagged with relief, sagged so much that Blank's men had to hold him up, and he began promising anything, anything.

Junior was so relieved that, once again, Blank thought the hippie might faint.

He hasn't realized that my men have not released his arm.

Blank stared into Junior's eyes, waiting, waiting, and then, with a speed and dexterity belied by his appearance, he lashed out with Miss Telstar and sliced the soft flesh of Junior's arm from elbow to wrist. He never looked down. The subject's expression was the best part as they realized what was happening.

At first, there was a thin red line, and then blood poured from the cut, running down over Junior's wrist, across the silly wide leather watchband and dripping from his fingertips into the sink, just the way it was supposed to. Tidy. Blank moved his face closer, leaning forward until he could feel the hippie's panicked exhalations. *This is the best part. The best part. When the shark bites.*

The phone rang. It was all right; the best part was over. Manny released the trembling Junior, answered on the kitchen extension, and then handed it to Blank. What Blank heard made him frown, and he stretched the cord and looked out the windows at the parking lot. He listened to what the doorman said, thought for a moment, and then hung up. He motioned Manny away from the semi-conscious Junior and whispered instructions. He smiled as he did. Then he started cleaning Miss Telstar. Tidy.

Junior Higgins stared at the blood running into the sink. Then his bladder emptied, and his eyes rolled up till only the whites showed. This time, he fainted.

Rider and Jane

Rider and Jane were sitting in Rider's Falcon in the convention center parking lot, out of ideas, when two Long Beach police cars showed up behind them, strobing their red and blue lights.

Jane turned around and saw Terry Griswald getting out of the passenger side of the first black-and-white.

Rider muttered, "There's a man with a gun over there."

Jane said, "It's okay. His name's Griswald. We . . . I know this guy. I've, uh . . ."

Rider looked at her.

She thought they were saved when Griswald walked up, but he said, "Step out of the car, please."

"Terry, I'm so glad you're here, I–" Jane stopped when she saw his expression and that the other cop was flanking him, hand on his weapon. The other uniform was standing behind the open car door. "What's going on, Terry?"

"You have the right to remain silent." The Miranda statement was new; he read it from a card he'd removed from his wallet. "You both are wanted for questioning for allegedly drugging a student named Deanna Mecum."

Jane stammered, "That's crazy. You know it's crazy. Deanna's my roommate."

"We have a written statement from her to that effect."

"That's not possible."

"She apparently dictated it shortly before being released from Long Beach Memorial. It took it this long to work its way through channels."

"It's a mistake, it has to be." *The key word there is "apparently." Terry's trying to tell me something. He doesn't trust the written statement. Maybe.* "Terry, I talked to her after she was released, and she was fine."

"Miss Bailey, these officers will take you both to answer questions. I volunteered to accompany them because you and I have spoken in the past."

"Who wants to talk to us?"

He ignored her question.

Rider spoke up, "Listen, this whole thing is a mistake."

An unmarked one-year-old black Chevy pulled up behind the police cars. Jane paused as the third car stopped next to the other radio patrol cars and two men in suits and hats got out. They walked over to Griswald, stood with their backs to Rider and Jane, and showed badges, and a few words were exchanged before Terry reached in and pulled the keys out of the ignition of Rider's Falcon. He handed them to Rider, and then he and the uniformed cops walked back to their cars. The two men in suits had gone back to their car and were sitting in it with their heads turned away, one talking on the radio.

Jane trotted after Terry and caught his arm. "Terry, wait, wait just a minute. You're leaving?"

"Change of plans. These gentlemen will interview you first."

There it is again. He's telling me something. What?

"That's what I have to talk to you about, what happened to Deanna. It's part of something bigger."

"These gentlemen will take your statements. I believe they are part of the federal agency that made the first approach to you. Of course, you would call them about this trouble."

Oh my God. He thinks I was in trouble and called the feds before him, and he's pissed. No, not pissed. Hurt. Like when he thought I set him up for the parking lot ambush.

"Terry." She grabbed his arm. "You know I didn't do it. I sure didn't give Deanna LSD, but even that's not important now."

"I'm sorry, Miss Bailey. You can sort it all out with these gentlemen." Terry and the uniformed cop got back in the black-and-white, the driver made a k-turn, and drove out of the parking lot. The second black-and-white followed.

But when they turned to face her Jane saw the men in gray suits and snap-brim hats were not the two Jane knew.

She heard her heart beat.

As the implications of what she saw became clear, she thought, *Run!* but there was no chance, and the same force that closed off her windpipe, clamping down with hot, dry fingers, also rooted her feet to the pavement. *They shouldn't be here.*

They had fooled the police. They had fooled Terry Griswald with a fake statement from Deanna. *We got in the way playing detective, so they swatted us.*

The two police cars, one with uniformed cops and the other with her friend – *date, Terry took me out* – turned onto Shoreline Drive. *I should have let him kiss me a second time.*

She heard her heart beat again.

I've faced worse than these guys.

"Hello, Miss Bailey. Jane. May I call you Jane?" the tall one said. They were the men who had chased them on the beach at the fire ring. They were the men who had pushed Terry Griswald's car into the dark corner of the parking lot. They were Blank's men. And the short one, the one she'd dubbed "Cigarette," was the one who'd held her and pressed against her that night in the field when she'd been cut.

"Where's your hippie wigs?"

Rider muttered, "Oh shit, it's them." He shifted his feet and clenched his fists.

"Don't need the wigs now. But relax, honey. We ain't gonna hurt you." He hooked his thumbs into his Sansabelt slacks and smiled.

Cigarette smirked. "Unless you do something stupid."

"Shut up. But it's true. You act up, well, we got permission to do whatever we need to. Dig?"

"Yeah, can you dig it?" The short one took out a Marlboro, rapped the filter on his watch, and lit up with a flick of his Bic.

The tall one reached up as if to take off his hat, changed his mind, and said, "I'm Manny. Rider, I've been instructed to tell you to lock your car. Somebody will bring you back when this is done."

He knows Rider's name. They weren't just watching us at the beach.

Rider said, "Really?"

"Just lock it, okay? Or don't for all I care."

Rider still had the keys in his hand. He carefully locked first the passenger door and then slowly walked around the car and locked the driver's side door, and as he did, Jane could sense him stalling, trying to think of something to do to get away. He gave up, looked at her to see if she had another inspiration like swimming through the red tide, and when she shrugged, he appeared to stuff the keys in his jeans pocket, but Jane could see he'd palmed them, wrapping them in his fist.

"I need my purse." Jane followed Rider to his car and whispered to him, "Don't do anything. This is perfect. We wanted to find stuff out, and now we will." Rider rolled his eyes but unlocked the passenger door so Jane could pick up her shoulder bag. Manny and his pal walked them over to their car. Jane noticed the bumper sticker and nudged Rider. It read: "If you don't like cops, the next time you're in trouble, call a hippie."

Rider grunted. He shifted his weight, and Jane could feel him getting ready to fight. She shook her head and murmured, "No."

Manny laughed. "Go ahead, kid. Take a poke at me. And while we go around, my pal will play with the blonde."

Jane almost changed her mind and did it anyway, jumped at Cigarette while Rider took on Manny. They'd expect it, of course, and she wanted this to look right. She saw they were both waiting for it – Cigarette ready, hands loose at his sides, grinning around the smoke he hadn't even bothered to put out, Manny with one hand in his front pocket, wrapped around something. *Brass knuckles?* She touched Rider's arm and shook her head again. It took him a moment to relax.

"All right, you two will ride in back." Manny had the door open.

And as they stepped toward it, Manny and his friend whipped out black cloth bags and slipped them over their heads, pulling them tight with drawstrings jerked against their throats before twisting their arms behind them and clicking handcuffs closed.

They were shoved into the back seat, and the door slammed. Jane was mostly stretched across the seat, half on Rider, who was crammed into the footwell. "You okay?" he whispered.

"Sure, I'm fine except for the handcuffs and the bag over my head," she whispered back.

"Hey, you two," Manny said. "We can hear everything you say." Since neither Jane nor Rider had anything of interest to say, they shut up and tried to squirm into more comfortable positions. The radio was on an oldies station. Manny and his pal sang along with Elvis telling them they had to follow that dream wherever it led them.

Time went by. They didn't know how much. Then the car slowed, bumping over something like a low curb. There was a grinding, metallic sound, they rolled forward, and the sound of the engine changed, echoing. The motor was turned off; the front doors opened and closed. The grinding noise came again. Jane moved so she was against Rider's head and whispered, "Garage door." She felt him nod. For a moment, they both wondered if they were going to be left in the car, handcuffed, with opaque black bags tied over their heads. Then the passenger-side back door was opened, and they were hauled out.

"We're not gonna talk!" Rider said defiantly.

A voice Jane thought was Cigarette's said, "I got nothin' to ask. How 'bout you, Manny? You got any questions?"

Manny responded, "Shut up. Look, we're gonna leave you here for a while." Jane felt a hand on her elbow. "Straight ahead. Walk." They guided Jane and, she assumed, Rider a few paces away from the car, turned her around, pushed her backward until she bumped against something that might have been the seat of a chair, and pushed her down. She sat. She heard Rider grunt as they shoved him down.

One set of footsteps moved away. Jane felt hot breath on her neck and shoulder, breath that smelled of cigarettes. Then a hand slipped down the front of her blouse and caressed her breast.

She whipped her head around, opened her jaws wide, and clamped down on the arm. True, her head was inside a cloth bag, but the human jaw can exert hundreds of pounds of pressure per square inch, and Cigarette – Jane was sure it was him because she could smell his Marlboros even through the bag – had taken off his sport coat, and Jane was extremely motivated.

He screamed and jerked his arm free. "Bitch bit me! Ow! Shit! Shit! She bit me!"

"Good. You deserved it. No more shit from you."

"But–"

"Fine by me. He won't mind that you didn't follow orders. Of course, he did say no messing around."

There was a moment of silence. Then: "Hey, Manny, c'mon, man, you ain't gonna tell him, are you?"

"No more shit from you."

"Yeah, yeah, sure, man, whatever you say. Don't tell him, okay? I think I'm already on his shit list after the beach."

"You are. Okay, you two, listen up. Here's what's gonna happen. Our boss doesn't want to hurt you, dig? So just hang out here. In a while, some friends of yours will come and let you go. Okay? Just be cool. I'm leaving the keys."

There was a whispered conversation and then the metallic jingle of keys being dropped onto a hard surface.

Manny's voice said, "We'll take the other car. Cops know this one."

"Sure, Manny, whatever you say." One set of footsteps moved away. From close by her ear, a voice whispered, "And you and me will get together later. Count on it, bitch." Another set of steps moved away, and Jane heard the noise she assumed was a garage door of some kind, footsteps, car doors slamming, a motor starting. The motor sound faded, and then there was the garage door sound again. Then it was quiet.

"Jane, what happened?"

"Shhh." She listened, heard nothing. She waited a little longer. Still nothing, except maybe a breeze, wind through – no. "Okay, that sounded like a garage door going down. I think they're gone."

"You bit one of them? Good. Any particular reason, or did you just feel like it?"

"He, you know, grabbed me."

Rider said softly, "The short one, wasn't it? He and I will have to have a little talk."

"Forget it. Now, let's see."

"Jane–"

"Shh."

Inside the bag, she closed her eyes and thought. She visualized what she'd have to do. Then she went over the steps again.

Okay, time to give this a try. One step at a time.

First, Jane half-stood and scooted her wrists under her butt, grimacing inside the hood when she sat on the handcuff bracelets and they dug painfully into her wrists. Then she pulled her knees up to her chin, worked her hands out from under her butt, pushed her feet together, and tried to slip her wrists past them, left, then right, then left again. *I can do this. It's going to work. It hurt more when I fell, when I fell in the – I won't go there.*

The chain caught on the heels of her shoes, so she had to work it free and pull it back before she could try to kick off her flats. When she slid her hands back, she lost her precarious balance on the chair and toppled over.

She had an instant of total fear as she fell sideways, unable to see, her hands bound under her and with no idea of what lay beneath.

She slammed onto a hard, cold floor, landing painfully on her left shoulder and hip. And the handcuffs were pushed back, once again under the seat of her pants. And her shoes didn't come off.

"Jane, Jane, what happened? Are you okay?"

She gasped, "Give me a minute," and lay still until she caught her breath and began again, pulling her knees up, kicking off her flats, trying to slip the chain down and then over her feet. Her shoulder was on fire, pain running up to her neck, down to her wrist and back again. *Hurts. I don't think it's dislocated. Of course, I have no idea what a dislocated shoulder feels like.* Then she could feel the chain on her heels and then on the arch of her foot. It was actually easier lying on her side. *Take note, class. When blindfolded and trying to move handcuffs from back to front, lie down on your side. There will be a quiz. Pass/fail. Also, wear capris.*

This time, she was successful, and she slipped her hands past her toes. For a moment, she just lay on her side, breathing, and then she squirmed up to a sitting position, reached up, and tried to pull the bag off her head – only to find that it was tied at the throat with some kind of cord and the knot was at the back. It was futile. While she could reach over her head with her hands cuffed, it was too awkward to untie the knot. She scooted to her right until she felt her chair. Then she pushed around in back of it, sliding to where she thought Rider's chair was. *These pedal pushers are ruined.* She would have missed it, but her bare toes brushed against one of the legs. She moved forward till she felt Rider's ankle.

"Jane, I really hope that's you."

"Who else?"

"This place might have rats."

"Glad you told me that."

Next she worked her way around to the back and groped until she found his hands. Then she turned her back and said, "Rider, you gotta untie the knot at the back of my hood. I can't reach it." She squirmed around until she could feel his hands at the back of her head.

"No problem, no problem. Scoot in closer, as close as you can." She could feel his fingers, uncertain at first and then working methodically. Then stopping. "Jane, the cord is tight."

"Tell me about it."

"I'm gonna have to get my fingers under it, pull it out so I can work on the knot. It's gonna choke you."

"Do it. We can't mess around. There's people coming."

"The tall one said they'd let us go."

"You believe him?"

Rider sighed. "No."

"Do it. Be quick."

She felt his fingers fumbling at the back of her neck, digging in and then pushing under the knot. The cord tightened. Just as she thought, *This isn't so bad,* it tightened again, digging in, clamping her windpipe shut, and cutting off any chance of air. Her first instinct, born of panic – *I can't breathe!* – was to raise her handcuffed hands to pull the cord out so she could breathe, breathe! She jammed her hands down between her knees and squeezed. She was dizzy, and her tongue thrashed uselessly against her teeth. She felt like throwing up, but she knew that would be very, very bad. Gray mist seemed to be seeping in around the edges of her vision, mixing with the dark from the bag.

This isn't working. I've got to tell Rider to stop. But when she opened her mouth, she found she'd waited too long – no sound came out. The moment of fear she'd felt as she'd toppled off the chair came back, and this time, it went on and on.

Now she did pull her hands out from between her knees, intending to push Rider away. *He thinks I'm okay. He doesn't know I can't talk.* This was too late too. The gray mist covered everything, and the world went away.

The next thing she knew, a voice was yelling, "Jane! Jane!" and she was lying on her side again. But the cord was loose. She could breathe.

For a moment, she just sucked in air. Then she reached up, slipped her thumbs under the bag, and pulled it over her head, feeling grim satisfaction as the damp spot her mouth had left when she'd bit Cigarette Breath slid over her cheek. Then she loosened the knot the rest of the way and dragged the bag off. For another moment, she just sat, breathing and listening. "I'm okay. I'm okay." Then she stood, almost falling as her left leg, the one she had landed on, nearly collapsed. She looked around their prison. It seemed to be a large, metal-walled building, windowless, oil-stained cement floor, with buzzing fluorescent lights suspended from the ceiling. The only thing in the warehouse other than their chairs was a car front of them.

"Oh man, I was freaked. I got the knot loose, but I heard you fall over, and you didn't say anything, and I just freaked."

"How long have I been out?"

"Wait, I'll check my watch. Oh gee, I have a bag over my head."

"Rider–"

"Not long. Five minutes maybe."

Rider was sitting in a folding chair, hands cuffed behind him, only his hands were pulled over behind the back of the chair. *If they'd done that to me, I don't think I could have gotten loose.*

"Get this bag off me." She quickly untied the knot and pulled it over his head.

"Wow," he said, gasping and blinking and looking at her wrists which were now handcuffed in front of her. "Girls really are flexible."

"Thanks. Now for the cuffs. I heard keys hit something. Manny had to leave them for whoever came back to let us go." Jane took a step forward, and at that moment, the lights went out. Rider said, "Perfect. Just perfect."

Jane, still shaky from the fall, jumped before she said, "Must have been on a timer."

"Yeah. Jane, it sounded to me like the keys landed on metal. Maybe the hood of the car."

"Makes sense. I think the car is in front of me." But she took a dozen short, careful steps, cuffed hands in front of her, and found nothing. To be sure, she stepped three more times. She stopped, disoriented by all that had happened and by the dark. Four more steps, this time to her right. Still nothing. "Rider, I can't find it, and I'm turned around. Talk to me."

"Yeah, okay, uh, hi, Jane, this is me, Rider, speaking to you from the total dark of some warehouse – at least, I think that's what it is. I think I saw an office or something off to my right. Anyway, it had windows that don't look outside. They look out into the warehouse or whatever this is, and there's a door, and shit, I don't have a clue what to say except that I really want to punch Mr. Cigarette in the face. I mean, he's my first choice, but right now, I want to punch anybody except you. Of course I don't want to punch you, Jane – and I can't see a damn thing and –" Rider stifled a scream as Jane put her hand on his face.

"Sorry, I'm sorry, Rider. I was trying for your shoulder."

He was panting like a dog that's chased too many Frisbees. "It's okay, sure, fine, yeah, I'm okay. Only a minor heart attack." With her fingertips on his neck, she could feel his pulse racing.

"I think I'm oriented now. Hold still."

"I'm not going anywhere."

She didn't answer. Instead, she put her back to his chair, pushing the back of her calves against his knees, straining to remember where the car – and hopefully the keys – were. She tried to steady her breathing and extended both hands in front of her even though her brief look at the warehouse before the lights had gone out had shown it to be empty. She took the first steps, sliding her feet across the cement floor in case there were obstacles she hadn't noticed. And then, as she slid her left foot forward for another step, it happened.

She heard the soft, secret whisper of wind through corn stalks.

She froze. Rider whispered, "Jane, you find it? Jane?" He laughed nervously. "And why am I whispering? This is Blind Baby Rider on KFWB talking to you from a dark warehouse and playing all the hits. Next up, Barry McGuire with 'Eve of Destruction.'"

At the sound of his voice, she would have screamed, but her throat was clenched tight. She could neither talk nor breathe. Tired and frightened as she was, the dark pressed in. *Not now, oh please, not now.* Her chest felt like it was wrapped in one of those metal bands she'd seen farmers put around bales of hay. *He's out there, out there in the dark, grinning his bloody, broken grin. Mess you up. Oh yes, he's out there. He's closer. Run. I have to run. He's closer.*

Being tied up, falling in the dark, choking, it was all too much. She closed her eyes only to see bright spots dancing across the inside of her eyelids, and it was hard to breathe. She could hear the wind in the cornstalks.

At last she sucked in air. She whimpered. "Damaged goods."

I can't breathe. I can't breathe because my throat is full of corn silk.

"Jane, Jane, what's wrong? Talk to me."

Dizzy. I'm so dizzy, like when Daddy swings me around and around as we dance and we laugh and laugh. "He's out there." She wasn't even aware of sitting down until the cement smacked into her left hand and bottom. She crossed her legs tailor-fashion and folded her hands in her lap.

"Who? Jane, there's nobody here but us and maybe a rat or two, and boy, I'm sure glad I said that, and Jane, talk to me, Jane, because I'm freaking out here again."

And all at once, it came pouring out. "A bad man. A bad man, and he came to our house, and he h-hurt Mommy and Daddy, and he was going to hurt me, but I ran into the cornfield, and he chased me, and then I killed him. I killed the bad man. I killed him, and I didn't even feel bad. There's something wrong with me. I'm damaged."

It was a child's voice.

Rider

Rider was speechless for a moment. He heard cloth rustle as she moved. "Jane, your parents live in San Francisco. You told me. I didn't think you meant it when you told me before about, about what you did, I mean, not exactly. I didn't know what to think."

"Not my real parents. Oh no. The bad man killed them, and then I killed him, and now he's here to kill me, and he's right, because I'm bad."

"Jane, Jane, how old were – are – you?"

"Next year, I'll be thirteen." Rider felt a chill wash over him. "I led him to the old well where the boards were over it, and I could step on them, but he couldn't, and the boards broke, and he fell down. He said mean things, and he was hanging on, and he asked me to help him, and then he said mean things, and then he fell. He asked me to help him. He asked me to pull him up. He said a lot of bad words, and then he fell. He screamed."

Rider had been crew team coxswain since his freshman year at Long Beach, and he did more than steer the sixty-foot-long eight-man shell; he was captain, coach, and cheerleader, goading the team along as the tall crewmen pushed with their legs, shot the slides, feathered the oars, and did it again till they were ready to pass out. And he could always get a Big Ten, ten more strokes, out of them.

"Daddy was a bookkeeper. He knew things about bad people, and when he told the police, the bad people sent the bad man to kill us."

"Jane, listen to me. You're twelve?"

"I had to live in safe houses, but sometimes they were apartments. The men in suits took me there."

Rider, old son, this is bad. The other shell has a boat length on us, and they're pulling away. You need to figure this out because Jane's right, the people who come probably won't be our friends, and something is going to happen at the demonstration. Eve of Destruction.

"I could hear the wind in the corn. It was whispering."

"Jane, how much do you weigh?"

"The wind was telling. It was telling what I did."

"Sure, sure. But how much do you weigh?"

"Daddy says I'm getting big. I'm almost five feet tall."

The voice coming out of the dark was still that of a child.

"Forty pounds?"

"Daddy says I'm too big to carry around. I weigh almost fifty-five pounds."

"Jane, listen to me. It's impossible. The bad man didn't want you to help him. He was trying to kill you. You couldn't have pulled him up t's impossible." Silence. "He wanted to pull you down with him. He wanted to kill you too. You've never told anybody about this, have you, not even the men in suits?"

"They wouldn't like me if they knew I was bad. Nobody would like me."

"All right. Now listen up. We're in trouble here, but that's not the worst. Blank's going to do something bad at the demonstration, and we're the only ones who know that. Jane, I know it's bad and it's dark and scary. I'm scared too, but the bad man's not out there. He's dead, and you didn't kill him." *Well, not exactly.* "You really didn't. Now you gotta help us. You gotta find that key. You can do it. If you don't, if you don't lots of people are going to get hurt, maybe die, and that *will* be your fault."

He could hear her breathing,

"So you had a bad childhood." *Okay, just about the worst childhood I've ever heard of.* "Get over it. If you give up now, everybody will be mad at you. I'll be mad at you. I'll never speak to you again. You can do it. Come on, reach deep, Jane. You're stronger than he is." *Say something, anything.* "The floor, Jane, feel the floor. It's cement – not dirt. Not a cornfield. Big Ten, Jane, you can do it."

That was it. Rider had played his last card. In the dark, there was only silence. He thought, *That rustling sound is wind blowing in under the door. Sure it is.*

"Okay, I'm here." It was her voice, her real voice.

He started to say something, but the tears in her voice stopped him.

He could hear her shuffling toward him. Then her hand once again found his face.

"Okay. The car's in front of us, I think."

"Sure, sure, Jane, it's right there, a few steps away. Ten, ten steps, and you'll find it. I'll count. One, two . . ."

"One, two . . ." She counted with him and bumped into the car on step nine. "I'm at the car. Now I have to be very careful. If the keys are on the hood, I don't want to knock them off because they'll be really hard to find on the floor."

"Right. Good thinking. Keep talking to me."

"The hood feels warm. I can't, you know, sweep my hands across it. I'm sort of lifting them up and putting them down. Nothing but hood. I feel the hood. I'm moving to my right. Okay, now I feel the door handle with my other hand." It was so quiet he could hear her breathing. "Rider, there's nothing. I don't feel anything. They must be on the floor."

If they are, she'll never find them in the dark.

"We heard them land on metal, maybe the trunk." He licked his lips. "Try again. Take it slow."

"Wait! Wait! I touched something! It moved a little. It's the keys, I know it is. They were in the groove where the windshield wipers go. I can feel them with my baby finger." For a moment, it was quiet.

"I got 'em! I got 'em! And Rider, thanks."

"I got 'em!" said Jane. *This might actually work.* She stood with her back against the hood. Ten steps later, she bumped into Rider.

She had just unlocked Rider's cuffs, groped for his hands to give him the keys, and extended her arms so he could unlock hers when the lights went on. Pleiades, flanked by Nowhere Girl, stepped out of the office, with Andromeda in the rear, hulking over the other BID girls. They all had weapons, two of them large wrenches, Andromeda a bicycle chain that she twirled casually. For a long moment, the whisk-whisk of the spinning chain was the only sound. Then Andromeda said, "Junior said we could come out here. He put us in charge."

Pleiades bobbed forward at the waist, nodding, holding her wrench in front of her chest. Her glasses slid forward; she thumbed them back and said, "In charge of you."

Nowhere Girl, of course, said nothing.

Jane stepped away from Rider. One handcuff was off, but the other was still around her wrist. She slipped her fingers through the loose cuff and held it down by her side.

"Andromeda, you need to let us go. It's really important."

The big girl grinned. Her muddy, close-set eyes sparkled. "I bet your parents never told you to learn to cook. We do this–"

"Out of love. I get it. But–"

"Just like I did your little princess pal."

Jane stopped. *I should have known.*

Pleiades stepped forward and took a swing at Rider. It was a mistake. The short-tempered coxswain had been handcuffed, stuffed in the back seat of a car with a bag over his head, and locked in a pitch-black warehouse with a girlfriend who occasionally thought she was twelve years old. He ducked under the swinging wrench, stepped in, and punched Pleiades in the face as hard as he could. Her nose and lip exploded in red, and she shrieked before dropping to her knees, covering her face, with an amazing gush of blood running between her fingers, over her arms, and dripping on the floor. As the other two turned to gape at their friend – clearly they had not expected this – Jane tripped Andromeda and, after the big girl went down, stomped her hand into the concrete floor, eliciting a very satisfying shriek that blended with her friend's. Jane snatched the bicycle chain out of the injured hand and, when Andromeda started to get up, hit her with it, catching her on the wrist and snapping the bone. She hadn't even had to use her improvised brass knuckles. Nowhere Girl was open-mouthed, staring, holding her wrench vertically in front of her like a dormie girl holding a candle at the traditional engagement ceremony. When Jane showed her the bicycle chain, her eyes widened, and she stepped back and dropped the wrench. The shrieking stopped, and the clatter as the wrench hit the cement echoed off the metal walls. Andromeda whimpered and held her wrist to her chest. Nowhere Girl simply sat down on the cement and folded her legs tailor-fashion, like a kid in a kindergarten class. Jane gestured with the bicycle chain, and the others sat.

"Okay, what are we going to do with them?" Rider said. "They won't all fit in the trunk, and we only have two sets of cuffs." He looked at the girls sitting on the oil-stained cement floor. One was holding her wrist and whimpering; the other was holding a bloody handkerchief to her nose. The third had both hands pressed to her mouth. "This is like one of those word problems on the SAT. You have three crazies that you need to restrain and only two sets of handcuffs."

They solved the problem by cuffing Nowhere Girl's left wrist to Andromeda's uninjured right wrist, and Pleaides's right wrist to Andromeda's left. That wrist was already starting to swell, so they had to put the cuffs on up around her forearm. Now the biggest girl, and the one both Rider and Jane judged to be the most dangerous, was cuffed on both sides.

"Okay," Jane said. "Here's what we do. And girls, don't for a minute think that I do this out of love." She and Rider tried to get them to stand, and when they refused, Jane solved the problem by pulling on the chain around Andromeda's broken wrist. The pain brought the big girl lunging to her feet, dragging her friends with her. Jane and Rider dragged the three over to the black-and-white police car.

When Jane opened the back door, she found her purse on the seat. Thoughtful kidnappers. Also, there were no door handles on the inside. Perfect. They loaded their prisoners in and slid into the front, with Jane behind the wheel.

She said, "The demonstration starts with a candlelight march from the lower campus parking lot up to the quad in front of the library. Then there's a sit-in. Somehow Junior's going to give them all acid." She put the key in and turned the car on. It lurched forward and died. Even as she'd said it, the plan had seemed unlikely.

Rider said, "A real buzzkill, I guess. Kids on acid. Some of 'em get arrested or flip out."

Jane shook her head. "We're missing something. That's not . . ." She stopped, searching for what she meant, and the realization dawned on her. "It's not bad enough. Whatever the plan is, it's worse than that." They looked at each other.

Rider turned to the three sprawled across the back seat. "All of you, listen up. What's Junior going to do?"

"Don't you wish you knew." Andromeda was clutching her injured wrist to her chest, stretching the other girls' arms out. Pleiades used her free hand to wipe at the blood still leaking from her nose while, of course, Nowhere Girl just sat staring at her knees.

Jane said, "Come on, this is important. Did Junior buy drugs from Thaddeus Blank?"

"Who?"

Rider said, "Right. Jane, you're right, we're missing something."

"You and your fascist tramp don't know anything."

Rider went on. "You, with the glasses."

Jane said, "Pleiades."

"Right. Pleiades, come on. Blank gets LSD from people he or his friends bust, gives it to Junior or–"

At the same time, Jane and Rider said, "He doesn't give much to Junior. He keeps most of it." They looked at each other, knowing that they had another piece of the puzzle.

Jane pursed her lips. "Andromeda, what's your major?"

"What? Sociology. What's it to you?"

"How do you like it?"

Andromeda shrugged. "A lot of it's establishment bullshit, you know, but some's pretty interesting."

Jane nodded sympathetically. "Where's the acid?"

"What acid?" Andromeda smirked, proud of her clever answer, and elbowed Pleiades, unfortunately hitting the arm being used to stanch the blood flowing from her nose, causing the hand to bump painfully. Her friend winced and kicked Andromeda. But the big girl's eyes had given her away.

The office held two desks with aqua linoleum tops, a gray four-drawer steel filing cabinet, and an open door that led to a filthy bathroom. Three purses lay on one desk, and next to the purses, they found a half-full box of sugar cubes with an eyedropper wedged in the side. Next to the eyedropper was a brown glass tube about an inch long with a cork in the top. There was about half an inch of liquid in the tube.

Rider lifted it to the light and looked at it dubiously. "How do we know it's real?"

Jane grinned. "Let's do a little experiment. Psych 101. Lab time."

After collecting the purses and the tube and hurrying back to the black-and-white, they showed the tube with liquid in the bottom to their prisoners. Andromeda's eyes widened. "Hey, that's mine. Leave it alone."

Jane carefully removed the cork, tilted the tube, and touched her baby finger to the liquid. Then she reached across Nowhere Girl to hold it out to Andromeda, who leaned forward and sucked on it greedily. Jane replaced the cork and stowed the tube in her purse before running to the bathroom and washing her hands. The only towel was crumpled on the floor next to the toilet, so she wiped her hands on her pants. When she came back, Andromeda was smiling and humming a tune Jane recognized: the beginning of "In A Gadda Da Vida."

Rider stared at the big girl, who didn't seem like she'd be any trouble now that her mind was moving on. Then he swallowed and looked at Jane before he continued. "Okay. It's acid. Junior's drugging the protestors. But how?"

Jane slammed the door. "Let's find him and ask."

They sat in the front, Jane on the driver's side, huddled together on the bench seat for a long moment, trying to think. Finally, Jane said, "We can't handle this ourselves. We have to tell somebody."

"Sure, like those so-called cops."

From the back seat, Andromeda said, "Manny. The tall one's Manny. He has really good shit."

Pleiades said, "Shut *up,* Andromeda!"

"I love you, Pleiades. You're beautiful." The big girl started humming again.

Rider went on. "The guys who kidnapped us and brought us here with bags over our heads and locked us in this deserted warehouse? Sure, let's call them."

"You're really hung up on the bag on your head, aren't you? Let's try to avoid them, okay?" Jane looked at the lever growing out of the steering column. "Oh man, I've never driven anything like this."

"Three on the tree. No problem. I can do it." Rider scooted over, and Jane lifted herself – she couldn't resist grinning as she sat on Rider's lap for a moment – and then settled on the passenger side.

They looked around and realized that the roll-up door to the warehouse was closed.

Rider started to get out. Jane put her hand on his arm. "Stay here. Watch our friends in the back. If the big one – Andromeda – starts complaining, stuff this rag in her mouth. I found it in the bathroom."

"My pleasure."

Andromeda, however, was otherwise occupied, smiling and humming.

Jane got out and trotted over to the door. For a moment, she stood there. Then she spotted an unlabeled red button on a metal box to the right. She shrugged and pushed it. Gears ground, and the door rattled upward. Rider pulled the police car up, Jane jumped in, and they were free.

They found themselves on a driveway leading to a deserted street running between gray, one-story warehouses. "Look!" Rider pointed at the top of a giant white object sticking up above the other buildings. "I bet that's the Los Altos Drive-In." Rider headed in that direction, and after one wrong turn that took them into a cul-de-sac, they were heading south on Bellflower.

Jane reached under the dash, groped around, and pulled out a microphone. "Hello, uh, hello?"

From the back seat, Andromeda said, more curious than afraid, "Where did that snake come from?"

Jane said, "Shut *up*, Andromeda."

"I love all of you even though you keep telling me to shut up. Why does everybody tell me to shut up? It's not nice, and you remind me of my grandmother."

"You gave her the acid."

"Hello? Hello? Is anybody there?"

"Jane, what are you doing? Are you nuts?" Rider tried to drive with one hand and grab the microphone with the other, but she held it out of reach.

"We need help. In the movies, they always go it alone, but this is too big for us. We can't stop it by ourselves."

"You realize that we don't know exactly what *it* is?"

"No shit, Sherlock. That's one of the problems. We don't know anything for sure. We could be wrong about the acid."

"And we're in a stolen police car?"

"Well, yeah, we are."

All at once, the stress of being held prisoner lifted. They realized that they were, indeed, sitting at a traffic light on Bellflower Boulevard in a stolen police car with three college girls handcuffed in the back seat, one stoned on LSD that they had given her, while Jane was carrying a tube containing more of the drug. They started laughing and couldn't stop.

Rider gasped, "We probably won't get a speeding ticket."

"Right. They'll just shoot us."

At the next stoplight, Rider wiped his eyes. "Oh man, and I was worried about graduating and getting drafted."

"See? Puts things in perspective, doesn't it?"

"And we've evaded arrest. On *Dragnet*, they say flight is evidence of guilt."

"Manny and his pal the Marlboro Man aren't real cops, so it doesn't count." Jane was fumbling under the dash, twisting knobs. "Hello? Hello?"

The speaker crackled, but no one responded. Rider groaned, pulled off on a side street, and stopped at the curb. "I think you have to push that button on the side of the mike. Why am I telling you this? Shit. Sorry."

"Oh." She pushed the button. "Uh, hello?"

A moment later, a voice said, "This is a police frequency. Get off the air."

"I need to speak to Lieutenant Terry Griswald of the Long Beach police."

"Now you have to let go of the button."

"—federal offense. Not for civilian use. Get off the air now."

"He sounds upset. Now you have to let go."

"Oh yeah."

"—offense carrying severe penalties—"

"Detective Terry Griswald. Emergency! Terry Griswald. Long Beach police. It's an emergency."

There was no answer.

For several minutes, they heard nothing but static. Then: "Griswald. Miss Bailey?"

"Yes. Terry?"

"—am I not surprised? Over."

"Terry, are you at the demonstration?"

There was a pause, then: "Miss Bailey, say 'Over' when you're done. Negative. I am not at the demonstration. What is your current location? Over."

"Terry, it's an emergency. Meet me—" She released the button and thought fast before pushing it again and growling, "Broderick here. Ten-something at the donut shop. Ten-four. Signing off. Over and out."

Nowhere Girl spoke for the first time. "Hey, you're not gonna send us to jail, are you? We haven't done anything."

The light changed, and Rider pushed in the clutch and pulled the shift lever toward him and down, dropping the car into first, still not sure where they were going.

"The school?"

"Not yet. Just go down the street to Bob's Big Boy."

"Sure, why not?"

"Please, please, my mom will kill me!"

Sounding like someone with a very bad cold, Pleiades muttered, "Ut up, Anquility!"

"You shut up! You just shut up! My mom called me last night, and she made my stepfather move out after she found out all the stuff I said about him was true, and she says she's sorry and I can come home, and I want to, and she wants me to. So screw it and screw you too, Olivia!"

Jane said, "Olivia?"

After some violent snuffling and blood spraying that seemed to clear her nose, she said, "My face hurts, and my name is Pleiades."

"Sure, honey. Tranquility, what's your name? Your real name."

Nowhere Girl sniffled. "Francine. Francine Zoliski. Andromeda is Beatrice Claypool, but Junior says we can't use those names."

Pleiades shouted, "You traitor!" Then there was nothing but shrieks and the sounds of struggle from the back seat.

Andromeda whispered, "The bats will get you for that. Or my grandmother will."

Jane said, "Andromeda, shut up about the bats, or I'll gag you. And I thought it was snakes."

"Them too! And I never liked you! I don't love you anymore, Jane. Jane, Jane, no family name. So there. Da, da, da da da dum dum."

"And the only rag I have is soaked in something nasty. Francine, what are Blank and Junior going to do? It's acid, right? At the demonstration?"

Without looking up, Francine said, "Junior's split the scene. He just got in his van and split, and he wouldn't tell us where he was going. And we're family!" Jane just watched her, waiting. "All right, yeah, it's the demonstration, but that's all I know, really. I'm sorry, I'm sorry. Please, I don't want to go to jail."

Jane twisted around on the seat. "Francine, you got any money for a phone call? Is there somebody you can call for a ride?"

"I can get a bus on Bellflower." She leaned forward in the seat, pulling her left arm, handcuffed to Andromeda's right, with her. The bigger girl tried to pull Francine's arm up to hit her, like when the big kid bully grabs the little kid's fist, punches him with it, and says something witty like, "Why do you keep hitting yourself?" But Francine was not Tranquility anymore. She used her free hand to slap Andromeda, hard. "Quit that! Just quit it!" she screeched. The big girl quit. She also quit humming Iron Butterfly's big hit.

Rider turned south on Bellflower and headed for the restaurant, carefully obeying all traffic laws. They actually passed a Long Beach radio patrol car, but the men inside paid no attention to them. When they got to the Bob's Big Boy parking lot, Jane unlocked the handcuffs and let Francine Zoliski – once known as Tranquility – go. She scuttled off, clutching her leather purse and holding her macramé shawl tight around her shoulders, only looking back once.

Jane told Rider to stay in the car and to keep the motor running. She smiled at him, got out, brushed ineffectually at the smudge on her left hip where she'd landed on the cement and where she'd dried her hands, and stood next to the police cruiser, trying to look confident. *Okay, this will work.*

A moment later, Terry pulled in, sliding the TR4 to a stop across three parking spaces. He got out and stood for a moment, hands on hips, just looking at her. He shook his head. Then he took out his Tareytons and matches and did the Amazing One-Handed Match Trick. Jane was determined to wait him out. Finally, he pulled the burned match off, dropped it, and shook his head. "Jane, this police car is stolen."

"First by some other guys and then by us, so it doesn't count. We recovered it and brought it to you."

From inside the car, Rider muttered, "Here come–"

"Rider," Jane began. "Terry, this is Rider. He's my friend. Rider, this is Terry Griswald, Long Beach police."

"—da judge. I believe it's important to look for humor in bad situations. Oh yeah, nice to meet you."

Griswald started to get out a cigarette and then realized he had one in his hand. "You seem to be driving this stolen police unit, and – oh man. Are those girls in the back seat handcuffed?" He grimaced, threw his cigarette down, and ground it out.

"Why aren't you driving a cop car?"

"I've been given some time off. Wingarten is mad because the order came from somebody very high up and they didn't ask him first, but I'm still off duty."

"Okay, look, the guy I told you about, Junior . . . Pleiades, what's Junior's last name?"

"Bite me."

"He's got some acid and is going to use it at the demonstration, and I think he's connected somehow to Thaddeus Blank. I think Blank's really behind it all. Those guys that took us away really work for him." Griswald stared at her, reached for a Tareyton, changed his mind, and put it back. Then he changed his mind again and lit up. "Sometimes they wear hippie wigs."

At last, the tall cop nodded. "Hmmm. Even with my contacts, I can't find out much about Blank. Very mysterious. Very rich and very mysterious, but with lots of important friends."

"If you're suspended, how come you were with those fake cops who kidnapped us?"

"Pretended I didn't get the suspension order. When those guys showed up with this statement from Deanna Mecum, I didn't like it, so I went along. And anyway, I'm not . . . Okay, yeah, I'm suspended."

Rider said, "'Don't worry, Rider, we'll call my cop friend, and he'll help. Oh, yeah, good, we'll have somebody official on our side, and everything will be fine.' Let's review. Manny and his pal, the guys who pretended to be cops, first dressed up as hippies and chased us with tire irons. Then they put bags over our heads and locked us in an empty warehouse. Then we got loose, grabbed these girls when they wanted to beat us up with chains and stuff, stole this car, and called you." He leaned forward and rested his head on the steering wheel. "Did I miss anything?"

Terry had him get out of the car, and they all walked a few paces away. "All right, you two need to tell me everything from the beginning."

Jane and Rider looked at each other.

"Like Rider said, some guys chased us on the beach–"

"Red tide."

"The water was glowing."

"They were the hippies who pushed your car in the parking lot except they had on wigs."

A moment later, Griswald shook his head. "And the only reason you have to connect Junior and Thaddeus Blank – a respected member of the community and a strong supporter of the police – is that you followed them both to the vicinity of the International Tower?"

Jane said, "I followed Junior down there but lost him. And another time, we followed Blank, and that's where he went, I think, in that area anyway."

"And?"

"That's when we lost him." Both men looked at her. "And that's where we got kidnapped by Manny and his pal, in the parking lot. You were there. And like I said, they were the ones who tried to drag you out of your car, and they chased us on the beach. And the girls looked suspicious."

Rider muttered, "That'll hold up in court. 'Your Honor, the girls looked suspicious. Lock 'em up.'" He groaned and then straightened and stood next to Jane, arms folded across his chest. "It was Blank's men. They were wearing wigs."

Jane added, "Hippie wigs."

"I actually agree, but that's because I have experience and training. However, I guarantee I am the only person who will see it that way. Okay, these girls you have illegally restrained are part of Burn It Down?"

Jane said, "As near as I can tell, they *are* Burn It Down, and it was self-defense."

Rider pointed. "The big one with the goofy look on her face had a bicycle chain." Andromeda smiled and gave a little finger wave. Pleiades elbowed her friend.

"Is that blood all over that girl's face? Never mind, of course it is."

Rider said, "We can explain–"

"No! Please don't explain any more. Jane, when we were first notified you were on campus, we got a call from a federal agency. If this is so bad, why don't you call them?"

"Terry, we're losing time. We need to go. The only reason for them to kidnap us is to keep us away from the demonstration."

"The feds?"

"All right. I called last night, and they didn't answer, okay? They're busy."

"Perfect. You've got no official standing. This dangerous radical commie-symp group consists of two hippie chicks and one guy."

Jane frowned. "That's another thing. We're missing one. Maggie Molyneaux is not around, and I'm worried about her. The girls beat her up because she was friends with me. And it's Blank. I know it is."

The tall young cop went on as if she hadn't spoken. "And just what do you think I'm going to do? Now that I have violated the terms of my suspension, associated with known radicals, and in general destroyed what little career I had left."

Jane's jaw dropped. "Well, gee, I don't know, Terry, isn't it your job to protect and serve? And anyway, if your career's ruined, what have you got to lose?" She decided that was a poor argument. "Never mind. Forget I said that. Let's get to the demonstration."

Rider spoke up, "Call out the National Guard or something."

"As a matter of fact, that's been done."

"What?" Jane said. "So quick?"

"I don't agree with the decision – not that I was consulted despite all my efforts – but as we speak, the Guard is on the way. When the protesters get up to the library, the Guard will declare it an illegal assembly and move them out." He paused. "LSD in the water?"

He turned and looked at the two water towers looming over the edge of the campus.

"Oh man," he said.

The penultimate piece fell into place. Jane and Rider looked at each other. She said, "We need to get there now."

Griswald looked around, eyes moving from the police car to his Triumph to Jane. "All right. We'll take it from here. I'll, I'll call Captain Wingarten. We'll send in–"

"No." Jane looked grim. "No. I can handle it. Just get us close. Use the cop car. I've got an idea."

"Jane–"

"Blank thinks ahead. He's called out the Guard, and he'll have paperwork. Terry, don't you get it? He's in charge. When we get there, he'll laugh at us."

"At the station, they said Seventh Street is down to one lane and Bellflower is full of protesters."

"And once we're there, we need to find – "

Rider said, "Junior."

Jane shook her head. "Blank. And Maggie Molyneaux."

Somethin' Happenin' Here: The Demonstration

Terry Griswald was right. Even in the police cruiser, they could not get far down Bellflower. So, when they could go no further, he bounced two wheels up onto the curb. Then Jane, Rider, and Griswald got out and stood for a moment, islands in the mass of students moving toward the university.

All around them there was excited, nervous talk. There hadn't been very many demonstrations at Long Beach, probably because it was a commuter school with the vast majority of its thirty thousand students driving in to search for parking, hurry to classes, and then leave for jobs, homework, or families, so this was new, and it seemed everyone in the crowd knew it was going to be big.

They could hear the chants from the main body half a mile away:

"Hey, hey, LBJ, how many kids did you kill today?"

"ROTC off campus!"

Griswald pulled Andromeda and Pleiades from the back seat. Andromeda tried to reach up with her free hand to touch his face, but he pushed her aside. "Listen to me. I haven't arrested you yet. I'm taking you up the hill with us. Maybe you can talk to this Junior person. At any rate, don't try to run."

"You're beautiful," Andromeda whispered and tried to touch his face again. Then she looked up at the sky and flinched. "Did you see that?"

She kept looking skyward as they joined the crowd streaming up the hill.

Candles, sandals and hair, odors of incense and peppermint, patchouli, and pot. And signs, signs everywhere, waving as young people spoke their minds and shouted slogans. Terry's suit and tie got a few odd looks, but none of the chanting, sign-waving kids did anything other than flash him the peace sign. The crowd noise dropped as they got to the quad in front of the library, where they saw two drab green Army busses pulling in off Seventh Street, rolling slowly down the turnaround between the library and the Humanities Office Building. Blank's Cadillac was parked off to the side with the trunk open and a tall serviceman bending over it.

Griswald muttered, "They're here already."

An officer stood next to the Cadillac. At first, Jane didn't recognize him; then he took off his cap and ran a comb through the sides of his shiny black hair. Thaddeus Blank was in uniform and, from the way the others deferred to him, in charge of the National Guard. He cleaned his comb, pocketed it, replaced his cap, and stood watching as soldiers filed out of the vehicles. The tall soldier was now lifting small boxes out of the limo's trunk and stacking them on the fender.

The Guardsmen milled around, waiting for orders. They looked like the kids they were supposed to control but with short hair and uniforms.

If the protesters had seen the Guard, either they didn't care or they weren't paying attention. Two with leather headbands passed out leaflets while a third in a black beret spoke earnestly to another group.

Next to the library exit, a group of three Long Beach policemen stood watching. As Jane, Rider, and Griswald stood between the protesters and the Guard, one of the policemen moved, and Jane saw Maggie Molyneaux sitting on the curb with her hands behind her back. *Well, I wanted to find Maggie and Blank, and there they are. Now what?*

Another truck rumbled up and lurched over the curb onto the grass at the center of the turnaround. Officers herded the Guardsmen into a line in back of the new arrival; doors in the rear opened, and as each soldier stepped up, he was handed a rifle and then one of the small boxes from the Caddy's trunk. They sat on the curb and began loading their weapons.

One of the Long Beach cops walked over and stood next to Griswald. Without taking his eyes off the crowd, he said, "Where'd you find them?"

"Bob's Big Boy. Why?"

"You want we should take 'em down to the station?"

"Huh? I mean, what?"

"Hey, we'll give you the credit. It'll be your bust."

"Sir, sir, I think that officer wants you." Jane pointed at the uniform who had pulled Maggie to her feet and now was standing with one hand on her elbow.

As soon as he hurried away, she said, "Terry, listen, I think he's talking about me and Rider. He wants to arrest us."

"Uh, what for?"

"Blank's done something, a warrant or something, I don't know, but he wants us. I told you he likes to think ahead."

"Oh hell."

"Yeah."

Then Blank stepped forward with a bullhorn.

"All right, kids, listen up. Quiet!" He waited a moment and then continued. "I am Colonel Thaddeus Blank, and I am in charge here." That got a few yells from the crowd, which he ignored. "Okey-doke. Now, this assembly has been declared illegal. However" – the crowd began to roar and chant – "however, I have some latitude. So, here's what we'll do. I'll give you some time. Make your speeches, sing your songs. Meanwhile, I will have my soldiers stand down for the time being. I have a canteen truck en route. My soldiers will have coffee and sandwiches, and when that is finished, this assembly is also finished. Is that fair? Sure it is. All right, soldiers, line up for coffee and chow."

Jane looked at Terry Griswald. "What the hell?"

He frowned. "Maybe this will all work out. Want some coffee?"

"They get their guns and – are those real bullets?"

"Looks that way. Live ammo? Maybe."

"And then they stop for a sandwich? That's nuts. No, no coffee."

Off to their left, the dormie girl from the pig party, wearing a paisley granny dress and a straw hat with a cartwheel brim and a wide black ribbon that hung down her back, was sitting cross-legged on the grass, playing her guitar and singing softly. Jane caught a few words of "We Shall Overcome." A few people were sitting around her, singing along and passing a bota bag.

Blank shouted again, "We'll give you some time. Make your speeches. We'll allow that."

A smaller panel truck pulled in off Seventh Street and parked next to the troop transports. Cigarette, now wearing brown cords and a gray CSULB sweatshirt, got out and opened the sides, revealing large silver urns labeled Coffee and Water.

The kid with the beret now had a bullhorn. "We're not leaving! Pigs off campus!" The crowd roared approval.

The soldiers grumbled, forgot about coffee and sandwiches, and a few hoisted their rifles. Blank was shouting something, but whatever it was, was lost in the noise.

Then, from the south end of campus, the direction of the library, there were more shouted orders, and the uniformed men formed into a line facing the demonstrators. They stood shoulder to shoulder and walked forward slowly. The protesters gaped, and finally a few of the people nearest the Guardsmen started running. Others stood their ground. One of the runners tripped over the girl with the guitar and did a face-plant on the grass. The kid behind him also tripped and put a foot through the girl's instrument. The singing stopped, and the mood changed abruptly from a kind of party to near panic. For a moment that stretched out, the Guardsmen and the protesters stood facing each other, both sides uncertain.

Jane muttered, "Where's Maggie?"

Other kids ran and then stopped with about ten yards in between them and the Guard.

Rider said softly, "I don't like this. It would be better if the kids just split."

Terry nodded. "They're not listening to Blank."

Andromeda and Pleiades had vanished. It didn't seem to matter.

Suddenly Jane was running toward the soldiers. Rider ran after her, followed by Griswald.

Jane skidded to a stop, facing a wide-eyed kid probably no older than she was who looked as scared as she felt and who could have been one of the guys from the pig party except that instead of carrying an ice chest full of beer or a Frisbee, he had an M-14 on his shoulder.

Rider stopped on one side of her, and Griswald on the other.

"There!" She pointed to where Maggie Molyneaux was standing, hands behind her back and with Long Beach policemen standing beside her. Jane looked at the boy with the gun who was in her way. "Please let me through." He shook his head.

Inspiration struck. Jane said, "I'm with him. Terry, show him your badge." The detective promptly flipped out his shield, and for a moment, she thought it would work, but then the soldier shook his head again.

Behind him, the policemen started walking Maggie toward Seventh Street.

Thaddeus Blank dropped the tailgate on the canteen truck and directed two soldiers to drag the canisters of water and coffee out, followed by a gallon jar of mayonnaise and sandwiches wrapped in clear plastic. Both crowds, students and soldiers, muttered, shifted, and first grew sullen and then angry.

Behind Jane and her friends, the chant rose again, louder, angrier.

Some of the soldiers started shouting back at the protesters.

Protesters formed their own line and linked arms.

Both sides began shouting through bullhorns.

"Line up! On the double! Two lines."

"Stand your ground! Stand your ground! This is a peaceful assembly, and we are within our rights!"

A few people started singing, "We shall overcome." The atmosphere was changing with every shout, every taunt; then something dark flew out of the crowd and splatted against an Army truck.

Rider muttered, "Dirt clod."

"This time." Jane looked around desperately.

The coffee truck was almost open for business. On the military side, Blank shouted, "Coffee's open. Stand down." A few soldiers were breaking ranks to get in line for a cup.

Griswald said, "Is Blank trying to help? Maybe he's changed his mind?" The first soldiers got their coffee and plastic-wrapped sandwiches and sat on the curb to eat.

Jane was ready to beg the young soldier, or run and see if she could make it, but at that moment, there was shouting, and two Guard officers were yelling at each other. Griswald flashed his badge again. "Soldier, let us through. The other officers are already here." Maybe it was the authority in his voice, maybe the kid was just tired and confused, or maybe he saw his buddies lining up for coffee and sandwiches. In any case, it worked. Jane, Terry, and Rider slipped past and ran to Maggie.

Griswald showed the cops his badge and asked what was going on.

"We were alerted to this one and some of her friends," said one of the cops. "They're dangerous radicals. Lucky we found her." He had a firm grip on Maggie's arm and gave it a little shake. The tall girl, wearing white jeans and a blue cowl-neck sweater, looked terrified.

Jane pointed to Blank. "Is he the one who told you?"

"Who are you, young lady?" The cop eyed Jane suspiciously, taking in the rumpled blouse and filthy capris.

Jane turned to Terry Griswald, pulled him off to the side. "Terry, don't let them take Maggie away, please."

He nodded. "They seem to be listening to me for now. I think they're glad to have somebody with some rank making decisions." He straightened his tie and turned to talk to the police now that the Guard had stopped moving forward. He looked at the cop holding Maggie and took her free arm. The cop nodded and let go of the one he'd been holding. "Miss Molyneaux, how is Junior going to get the LSD up the water tower?"

Maggie looked at Griswald pityingly. "The water tower? Climb up there? That's silly. It would take too much acid and anyway. LSD breaks down fairly easily."

Jane said, "Maggie's a chemistry major."

Maggie nodded. "The water tower was never the plan. He's passing it out right here at the demonstration."

Jane said, "And it was never Junior. Blank used him. Blank's got the acid."

Griswald's eyes widened. "He's going to give it to the kids. Kids on drugs."

"And even if people figure it out, well, everybody knows the SDS wants to dump acid in the water supply." Jane stopped and thought a moment. And all at once, she got it, understood just how bad it was. She clutched Griswald's arm. "Maybe a little to the kids, sure. But he'll give most of it to the Guard. Kids on drugs with guns."

Maggie said, "I swear I didn't know until a little while ago. I ditched the BID girls and came here to tell somebody." She looked at the uniforms who had almost arrested her. "But somebody else had told them I was a dangerous radical who needed to be locked up."

Jane said, "Blank likes to think ahead. Coffee and sandwiches."

All at once, a campus cop was shouldering through the students, his eyes fixed on the soldiers. Jane saw the campus cop say something to one of the soldiers. The

Army guy responded; the cop shook his head. There was some arm waving on both sides. Then the unarmed campus cop stood in front of the soldiers, hands on hips.

Then Terry was next to Jane, with Maggie in tow. He took Jane's elbow and whispered, "This is bad."

"No shit, Sherlock, and now it's getting out of hand. They're not listening to Blank anymore." Jane paused, thinking. "It's all Blank. He faked the call that brought out the Guard, pretended to be Long Beach police asking for help. I bet he planted the statement from Deanna, the one that said I gave her the acid." Terry nodded. "And by the way, thanks for coming with us." She looked around and murmured, "We need a distraction."

The campus cop stepped close to the National Guard officer again. He spoke softly, intently. Finally, the officer shrugged and waved his soldiers back. But before they could move, another one of the officers was showing the campus cop a clipboard with official-looking papers. The cop looked at them and began to move to the side.

Blank poured himself a cup of coffee from a silver thermos and sipped.

He's thought of everything. Jane thought hard. Behind her, the crowd moved uncertainly, nervous now. She could hear them murmuring, for a moment like the sound of a breeze in a cornfield. *Manny and Cigarette are out there somewhere.*

Jane whispered, "Rider, that pea coat on the ground over there. Grab it."

"You want me to steal somebody's coat? Sure, why not?" But he tossed those words back over his shoulder as he trotted over to the coat lying on the ground and snatched it up.

Jane shook a few blades of grass off the thick blue coat, put it on, and hurried over to the guitar girl, who was sitting holding her ruined instrument and softly crying. "I'm really sorry about your guitar. Uh, can I borrow your hat?"

"What?" The blonde girl wiped her eyes, smearing her mascara even more, but nodded and handed it to her. Jane tucked her hair up under her hat, made sure the little tube was tucked into her waistband, took a deep breath, and went to talk to the men in uniform.

This will work. This will work. I hope this will work.

Two Long Beach policemen were trying without success to keep students who were coming out of the library away from the Guard and the protestors. Their backs were to Jane as, head down, she skirted them and slipped behind a six-wheeled Guard truck. She started working her way toward the pick-up with the water and the coffee. Then she stopped when she saw two men sitting on a bench and expertly loading their rifles. Manny and Cigarette. And they were between her and the canteen truck. *At least they haven't recognized me.* As the thought passed through her mind, she fully expected it to jinx the whole thing; they would look up, see her, and stop her. Maybe they'd shoot her. She pulled her hat down, hunched her shoulders, and tried to look inconspicuous.

One of the protesters with a bullhorn had mounted the stairs of the nearest liberal arts building, and leaning out over the railing, he started to exhort the crowd.

Both crowds were listening, the students raising fists in salute and the soldiers starting to group together. A few more of them shouldered their weapons. The kids swarming out of the library were shoving past the campus police and joining the protest.

Jane beckoned, and Rider and Griswald trotted up next to her. "Rider, see those two guys? Recognize them?"

"Oh yeah."

"It's time for you to have that talk with Cigarette."

Rider pulled his lips back over his teeth. "My pleasure."

Before they could get there, Manny handed his pal a small revolver and gestured to the crowd. Cigarette passed his partner the rifle, tucked the pistol into his belt, pulled the sweatshirt over it, and trotted into the crowd.

And before she could scream, "No, no, Rider, wait, he's got a gun!" the coxswain ran after him. They both vanished into the mob.

Jane groaned, tugged at the waistband of her Capris, and then grabbed Griswald's arm. "Listen, I can fix this, but if I do, will you make sure Maggie doesn't get charged with anything?"

"I don't see how anybody can stop this."

"She goes free, all right?"

"What can you do?"

"This is no place for a girl, right?"

At least he had the decency to blush.

"Listen, we're out of time. Blank's guy Manny is handing out live ammunition, and his pal Cigarette is in the crowd pretending to be a student, and he's got a gun."

"Oh man, I've gotta talk to the Long Beach cops."

"Will you get Maggie off?"

"Yeah, yeah, if I can, okay. What are you going to do?"

"Talk to Blank."

And before he could stop her, Jane was working her way around behind the coffee truck. She slipped up next to Thaddeus Blank for what would prove to be their next-to-last conversation. "You need to stop this, please."

It still looked somewhat under control: the Guardsmen were grumbling at the name-calling but forming into lines, some loading weapons, some exchanging words with the students, but there was no pushing or shoving yet, just clumps of young people in uniform and out.

Then, all across the lawn, the sprinklers turned on.

After a moment of surprise, the protesters started yelling, collecting possessions, and running, while the Guardsmen, safe from the spray on the paved turnaround, laughed and cheered. Instant chaos. Just add water.

Blank looked surprised when he saw her, but he recovered quickly. He set his cup on the truck's fender. "It's much too late." He gestured to the running students and spraying water. "Not bad, eh? I have keys for the timer. In fact, I have keys for everything." He chuckled again and glanced at the sky. "Any minute, this situation will explode, and the drug-fueled Communist Menace will be revealed, and I'll be a hero." He pulled out his little notebook, wet his thumb, and flipped through pages. "All right, okey-doke. One's due overhead but not for two hours. I'll be gone by that time. Have a cup of coffee."

Behind them, the protesters, now angry, shook fists, formed into a solid mass, and began to advance on the Guard. The sprinklers sputtered and then stopped, but the damage was done.

"You sent Cigarette into the crowd with a gun." Blank shrugged. "People could get hurt. Killed. Kids."

Another shrug. "Hippies and Communist drug fiends. The shark bites. Yes, it bites."

Keep him talking. "I thought about it, and you may be right. But one's due overhead in – what time do you have?" He just stared at her. *Keep him talking.*

Try again. She felt her mouth go dry. *One more chance.* "I talked to one of my professors. You're right. They could be spying on us." Now he was paying attention, focused on her. "There's a new one, Soviet of course. What time do you have?"

"Why do you keep asking about the time – oh! Now?"

"Yes, I think so. A new one." Blank frowned, but he didn't answer the question, instead pulling out his little notebook. "It's due now, moving east to west. Watch the skies."

Now he looked up, searching, pulling Miss Telstar out of his pocket and rubbing his index finger along the ivory handle. "I saw it one night in the sky as it passed over our house. They're winning. If they rule space, they rule the world. I'll stop it, and I'll be famous. People will love me, and I won't be afraid anymore. And you'll be famous too, not as famous as me, of course, but well-known, because I'll tell everyone how you helped me. I like you. I really do." He patted her shoulder, fatherly. "What did it mean? Oh, it was looking for me, of course. They'd love to stop me, oh yes. But they don't know the plan. No one does but me."

"Well, see, this professor believes the same thing, and now you've got support, so you don't need to do it."

He seemed to think a moment. "No. No, in fact, that's bad, because he'll try to take the credit. Oh yes, thank you for warning me. Okey-doke. Full speed ahead." He looked at her suspiciously. "No one knows. Have some coffee."

She hooked a finger into her waistband.

"Sure. Can I have some of that?" Jane nodded toward Blank's thermos. She took a Styrofoam cup off the stack next to the coffee canister and held it out. He smiled knowingly, ignored the thermos, and drained a little coffee from the canister into her cup.

"No, no. Here, try this. It's good. Fresh."

She looked up at the sky, searching for a moving spot of light. He couldn't help it: he looked too.

She did it.

"Now. Drink some coffee. I'll think about what you said." He drank the rest of his cup.

"Sure." She raised the cup to her lips. She drank.

He smiled. "Okey-doke. I thought about it, and the plan goes ahead. We stick to the plan. Of course we do." She wavered, stumbled into him, spilling coffee. He smiled, patted her shoulder. "You're not going to upset the plan now, are you?"

She turned and ran.

With her lips clamped shut, she ran back to the students and sprawled on the wet grass.

In a moment, she staggered back to Griswald. "Have you seen Rider or the guy he was chasing?"

He shook his head. "Lost them in the crowd. Don't know what we can do. Sorry, Jane."

"Rider! My friend Rider!" She took a deep breath. "Right now, we have to find my friend Rider. He's in the crowd looking for one of Blank's men, but the guy he's chasing has a gun and . . . I sent him, so if something bad happens, it's my fault. Uh-oh. Check out Blank."

The chubby man in the uniform was waving his arms, perhaps trying to direct traffic, but no one was paying attention. Suddenly he threw down his Army cap, picked up the giant jar of mayo, turned, and sprinted to the nearest classroom building, where he started running up the stairs.

When Griswald turned his back, Jane ran into the crowd.

She pushed her way through the protesters, stumbling, feeling the mood move ever closer to violence, looking for Rider, looking for Cigarette, looking for Rider. Somebody elbowed her in the ribs, said, "Hey, watch it," and vanished.

Why was Cigarette dressed as a student? Why did Manny give him that gun and send him into the crowd? Where is he?

All at once, she got it. She started pushing, shoving her way toward the Guardsmen, and there they were, Cigarette staring in Manny's direction – *waiting for a signal* – with Rider a few steps away and closing fast. The coxswain took a swing at Cigarette, who blocked the punch and knocked him down before reaching under his sweatshirt.

And I'm too far away.

Rider bounced to his feet and, before Cigarette could get the gun out, hit him three times in the face and once in the gut. Cigarette went down, still conscious, still fumbling for the gun, so Jane ran up and kicked him in the nuts as hard as she could. He made a noise like a teakettle at full boil, curled up, and lost interest in anything beyond clutching at his crotch. She bent and took the revolver from him.

Rider stared at it and said weakly, "Didn't know he had a gun."

"Keep an eye on him, okay? I don't think he can, ah, walk."

"My pleasure."

She trotted back to Griswald.

Two men in gray suits pushed their way through the crowd, flashed ID at Griswald, and stood next to Jane. She pointed at the Liberal Arts building Blank had dashed into. "He went that way." One of the suits turned and started speaking urgently into his walkie-talkie.

Jane said, "Maybe a better question is what's he doing up there?" Blank had appeared on the roof of the building. He had divested himself of coat and shirt. "Oh, look, now he's taking off his pants."

"Yeah." Griswald looked at Jane. "Has he been smoking some of those funny cigarettes?"

"Don't look at me." She batted her eyes.

Shirtless and in his boxers, Blank began waving his arms and singing to the crowd, "I can see for miles and miles!"

Jane grinned. "There go the undershorts."

The crowd noticed the chubby naked man who was singing. The frat guys – at the demonstration in the hope of picking up hippie chicks who believed in free love –cheered.

There were more scattered cheers and then growing applause.

Blank had another verse. "Hello, I love you! Here I come, gonna flash my – I love you all!" He started jumping up and down. "Look, look! I'm waving! Yoo hoo! I love you all!"

Griswald grabbed Jane's arm. She grinned. "You wanted a diversion."

The taller of the two men in gray gestured at the naked man on the roof. "Nice work."

She grinned. "Yeah, I had to do something, no, I mean, who me? And anyway, this is what you wanted."

"You knew." The man in the suit didn't sound particularly surprised.

Jane nodded. "Took me a while, but I think I get it. He's a cop, or he used to be one, still with friends in law enforcement, so he was untouchable but dangerous. You used me to bring him out, knowing that he'd try to get information from a Long Beach informant. Terry, these two gentlemen are feds. I don't know their names."

"You've been working with them without telling me."

"This is Detective Terry Griswald, LBPD. He's been a huge help."

"You didn't tell me!"

"I know, Terry, I was—"

"Miss Bailey, no."

"—not sure until a little while ago." She looked at Blank again, who now seemed to be doing a version of the Swim to music that only he could hear.

Suit Number Two said, "He was a threat, but our agency had no official interest."

Suit Number One said, "In point of fact, there were certain people who actually sympathized with him, so we, ah, folded it into the BID investigation."

"I can explain everything, but later. All of this will work out, and you guys will be heroes, but I want something in return."

"Miss Bailey, we're not in the habit of making deals with teenage girls." Suit One sounded amused. His partner was watching the naked man on the roof.

"I could go public."

Griswald muttered, "Heard that before."

Suit One didn't look concerned. "But in this case, we might make an exception. What do you want?"

"Maggie Molyneaux. She goes free. No charges, nothing on her record. Deanna Mecum. The drug event drops out of sight. No record."

He didn't even look at his partner. "Done. Now talk."

Everybody looked at Jane. She said, "He needed a major incident, even if he had to create one. Blank wanted to galvanize people into fighting the communists and to make him famous."

Suit Number Two said, "We really need to get some men up on that roof."

Now the soldiers were cheering too, putting their weapons down and laughing. One shouted, "Hi, Colonel! Do the Watusi!"

On the roof, two Long Beach police appeared behind Blank, but he was surprisingly agile; he turned and ran and reappeared a minute later on the third floor at the top of the stairs. He waved to the crowd before he disappeared inside the building, and then he reappeared on the second-floor landing.

Suit Number Two was yelling into the walkie-talkie again. "Where the hell are you idiots? Can't you grab one naked guy?"

The voice from the walkie-talkie said, "Sir, it's hard, I mean difficult. He's, well, he's all slippery."

"Slippery."

"He's got grease or something all over him." As they watched, a uniformed officer latched onto Blank's arm and slid off.

Blank shouted, "Hey, girls, watch this!" turned and straddled the banister.

Jane murmured, "Bad idea if you're naked."

Blank yelled, "Okay, here I go!"

Hippies, frat rats, and soldiers yelled encouragement. The campus cop refrained from cheering, but he could not hold back a grin. Slow at first, Blank started to slide down the metal banister. Almost at once, he was yelling, "Ow! Ow!" as he picked up speed and was trying unsuccessfully to stop. But whatever he'd smeared on his body was making his banister slide one for the ages. He rocketed down to ground level, off the end of the railing, and flew backwards until his feet touched down, and then he did two reverse somersaults before tumbling to a stop. He lay still for a moment, flat on his back, before staggering to his feet. Stumbling, clutching his crotch with both hands, he still managed to evade two more men in suits. He ran out onto the grass into the no-man's land between the National Guard and the students, tripped, and fell on his face. Two protesters and three Guardsmen reached him and were laughing and holding him up when men in uniform appeared and took his arms. The crowd pressed in, hippies mingling with straights and uniforms, all wanting a look at the crazy naked guy. Jane saw one of the Guardsmen give his jacket to a wet, shivering girl in a thin blouse and wondered, *Do I have her coat?* Then the suits pushed through, flashed IDs, and brought Blank over to where Jane's little group stood. Other uniforms were loading Manny and a stumbling Cigarette into cars driven onto the grass.

Blank kept looking up at the sky, now terrified. Then he sagged in the arms of his captors and looked up at Jane.

"Am I going to die?"

So tempting. Oh, that is so tempting. "No. But I wouldn't plan on operating any heavy machinery for the next few hours." She grinned.

He looked up at one of the men holding his arms. "I feel funny. We need to get under cover. One's coming over soon." He looked at Terry Griswald and whispered, "Don't let it see me."

"Sorry, chum."

He was dragged away, cowering, looking up as if things were coming out of the sky to attack him. Maybe they were.

And in the End

Saturday night, they met in the dorm cafeteria for a post-mortem. It was steak night, and for five dollars, guests Terry Griswald and Maggie Molyneaux got to enjoy a well-done hunk of meat, peas, and all the fries they could eat. Dining with Griswald were Rider, Maggie Molyneaux, Deanna, and Jane. Jane would have invited the suits, but they had vanished, and the phone number she had was disconnected. After they'd eaten and Rider had returned to the table with a second huge helping of fries, Jane took a sip of water and said, "All right, Detective Griswald, you're on."

Terry had found the dorm coffee undrinkable. He lit a Tareyton one-handed and leaned forward to use his coffee as an ashtray. "Okay, this is interesting. You were right: Thaddeus Blank was a cop, but he spent too much time recruiting for the John Birch Society. First, the cops warned him. Then they suspended him. Then they fired him. After that – and get this, only somebody with my sources could have dug this out – after he lost his job, the Birchers kicked him out, and that says something about how weird he was."

He tapped more ashes into his coffee. "He was freaked about the Soviets being ahead of us in space. It seems to have started when Sputnik I went up. His parents live somewhere in the Midwest, and they're rich – oil, I think – so he didn't need to find a job after the cops fired him."

"What about the LSD?" Jane had dressed for dinner in a pink tent dress, stockings with a wide fishnet, and heels. She sat between Rider and Griswald.

"We were wrong about that. It wasn't stuff he confiscated from dealers. He made it. He actually confiscated chemical instruments and supplies, everything he needed. We found it set up in the spare bedroom of his apartment in the International Tower."

Maggie said, "I was there once when Blank had Junior and the girls over for a lecture on the international Communist conspiracy. There was one bedroom that was off-limits."

Jane said, "Speaking of Burn It Down . . ."

Terry said, "Pleiades turned herself in. She thought jail was better than being handcuffed to Andromeda on drugs."

Jane grinned. "Makes sense."

"And Junior was picked up at the border, trying to get into Tijuana. He was babbling about Blank being crazy, but they found a dozen LSD tabs hidden inside a stuffed armadillo, so he has his own problems."

"Blank?"

"I think he's undergoing psychiatric evaluation as we speak. He's still pretty scared."

Rider, proudly sporting a black eye, snorted. "I can evaluate him," he said. "Batshit."

Jane poked Griswald. "You *think* he's undergoing evaluation?"

"Your friends the suits have him somewhere. Along with the psychiatric evaluation, he's being treated for, ah, abrasions."

"What about you, Terry? You were in trouble there for a while."

"Thanks for reminding me, Jane. Yeah, but my superiors, realizing my value to the department, have decided to forgive and forget. Plus, my suspension just appeared. Like, nobody's taking credit, so it's hard to enforce. I'm guessing one of Blank's cop contacts forged the papers."

Jane snagged one of Rider's fries, dunked the end in ketchup, and ate it thoughtfully. "Okay, and I bet the same is true of the orders to send in the Guard."

Maggie said, "And the order to arrest me."

Griswald nodded. "Right. It all looked official, but nobody in Sacramento knows anything about the call to the Guard. And I can't find anything about your arrest order because there wasn't one. Same with the order to arrest Jane."

Jane shivered. "He wanted to freak out the Guard, cause something really bad. He sent Cigarette into the crowd with a gun. The idea was he'd shoot one of the soldiers, and then Manny would shoot back. At least, that's what I think, but Rider took him out before he could."

Rider grinned. "He had it coming."

"Can't argue with that." Griswald laughed. "His real name is Elwood Brooks, and he's rolling over on his pal Manny."

Rider said, "No loyalty."

"Not after we told him Manny had orders to put a bullet in him after Brooks shot one of the Guardsmen. Blank felt like he'd outlived his usefulness. At least, that's what the suits told us, and we told Elwood. It might even be true."

Deanna said, "So why did that big girl–"

Jane filled in, "Andromeda."

Terry said, "Whose real name turns out to be Beatrice Claypool."

Deanna took a Virginia Slim out of her purse; Terry lit it, and she said, "Okay, why me? Why did she give me acid?"

"They wanted me to report it, Deanna, and it worked. Blank needed a pattern of incidents leading up to the demonstration." Jane looked down. "My fault."

Terry said, "Cut it out. Blank had his plan. You stopped him. I just wonder how he happened to drop acid at the demonstration." He looked directly at Jane.

"He's a very strange guy," Jane said. "I can see him doing drugs."

"And you vanished for a while there."

"I didn't feel well."

"Hmmph. Right." Terry tossed his cigarette into his coffee cup.

After the fries were polished off, Deanna, Terry, and Maggie left.

Jane stood up, but Rider pulled her aside. "Jane, I need to tell you something. I-I've met a girl. She's in Shell and Oar, and, well, and–"

"Rider, it's okay, really it is. We had a good time, and I'm glad you found somebody. It's cool, honest." And the awful time when the past had almost claimed her and he had seen her innermost secret, that was between them, at first a bridge, now a barrier.

Mary Jane Bailey met it head on. She touched his cheek. "Big Ten, Rider. I'll never forget."

"Yeah, that's, well, Jane, that's part of it, yeah. I was scared shitless – sorry – and, and you were having a good time. Well, for most of it." He nodded, hesitated, and then stuck out his hand as if to shake. She grabbed him and hugged him, hard, pulled back, and kissed both cheeks, gently on the side with the shiner. He flushed.

"If she's ever mean to you, I'll scratch her eyes out."

When Jane was walking out of the cafeteria, she saw Rider holding hands with a cute brunette, a cute, short brunette.

She turned left and headed down the hill to Cerritos Hall by herself.

Terry Griswald was waiting, standing in the parking lot next to the Triumph. "Broderick."

"Detective. What are you doing here?"

"Trolling for cute co-eds."

"After everything you did?"

"Found one too. I'm too groovy for you to let get away."

"Groovy? You really said 'groovy'? And you're out here looking for co-eds?"

"Wanna see the Amazing One-Handed Match Trick?"

She handed him her books. "I want to drive the Triumph."

"I want to know how Blank got the acid."

"I'll deny all of this." He shrugged. "Okay. I had the loaded tube we found in the warehouse shoved under my waistband. When Blank looked up for the satellite, I dumped it in his cup."

"But he gave you coffee from the urn, coffee that was drugged."

"A test. He was making sure I didn't know."

"And you knew, and you drank it anyway." She shrugged. "And then . . ."

"Yeah. Stuck my finger down my throat. Not very ladylike, but it worked. Hey, I've picked a major."

"Yeah? What?"

She looked at the badge clipped to his belt and then at the car.

"Wonderful. Okay, but be careful. Second gear is synchro, but you don't want to over-rev, and . . ." Then he paused and grinned. "Baby, you can drive my car."

"Gimme the keys."

In a few weeks, finals were starting, and after that, the cycle of semesters would begin again. And despite the horror of the war, always the war, there was a certain amount of laughter. Because it has to be that way.

Please don't throw toothpicks in the toilet.
Crabs can pole vault.

> – Graffiti in Fine Arts 1 Men's Room complete with
> an illustration of a grinning insect pole vaulting.

The End of *Buzzkill*
Mary Jane will be back in *Roachclip*.

About the author

James R. Preston spends most of his time at the keyboard, writing the award-winning Surf City Mysteries—think "beach noir." *Sailor Home From Sea* is the fifth novel in this series and was preceded by *Leave A Good-Looking Corpse, Read 'Em And Weep, The Road To Hell,* and *Pennies For Her Eyes.*

The Surf City Mysteries have been selected for inclusion in the California Detective Fiction collection of the Bancroft Library, one of the libraries at the University of California, Berkeley. You can read the opening chapter of each book at JamesRPreston.com.

Away from the keyboard, James likes reading, films (especially 1950's SF like *Them* and *The Crawling Eye*), sailing, bodyboarding, and Texas Hold'Em Poker. James played in one of the 2011 World Series tournaments and sadly busted out early. This year will be different.

Read 'Em And Weep

From the journals of T. R. Macdonald:

I was sort of hiding from two guys who either thought we were in business together or who wanted to kill me.

"Sort of hiding" because I could have left town and been relatively safe, but Las Vegas, NV, has so many wonderful things to see and do that I decided to go to a topless rollerskating show instead.

"Sort of hiding" because I was fairly sure that the guys in question would take Door Number Two and try to shoot me, a lot.

Why me? I'm T. R. Macdonald, a sort-of unemployed broker-analyst from the boutique—we handle a small number of very rich clients—firm of Fields, Smith, and Barkman. My sort-of girlfriend, Kandi, had asked me to go to Vegas to see if we could talk to her cousin Chet, because she thinks his adoptive father, Dr. Woodrow Shaw, may be nuts. Are you getting all this? There will be a quiz. Dr. Shaw asked me to go, too, and he offered to pay.

It sounded like easy money.

So I went.

I must be nuts.

The Road To Hell

From the journals of T. R. Macdonald:

I was standing in the desert, in the sun, outside of a semi-abandoned church, and I had a gun. My girlfriend, the lovely blonde Kandi Shaw, and I were registered in the Maiden's Blush Suite, one of the finest in Las Vegas' lavish Bromeliad Resort and Spa. Unfortunately, I wasn't in the suite. I was standing in the sun, waiting for my brains to finish boiling.

I'm T. R. Macdonald, a semi-unemployed broker-anaylst from Huntington Beach, California—Surf City, USA. And I was here instead of sitting on my short tri-fin outside the break line at the Huntington Pier because the casino offered me money to assist in security for WillieFest One, the richest slot tournament in history.

But so far I'd been mainly a moving target or punching bag—I was run off the road, chased by pit bulls, mixed it up with a vicious pimp, and was nearly trampled in a club stampede. Not to mention the part where I was poked in the nose. With a sawed-off shotgun. All of that led to the church, and my gun, and Kandi standing next to me with her gun in her hand—and she wanted to shoot somebody.

And if the two men inside the church didn't listen to reason, I was very much afraid she was right—I'd have to shoot them.

Pennies For Her Eyes

From the journals of T. R. Macdonald:

I was sitting on a wet bike in frigid water, watching waves the size of three-story buildings slide toward me, hump up, then hump up again getting even taller before crashing down with a sound like a Las Vegas casino imploding. I could be in one of those casinos, a fancy one, too, because they liked me and wanted me to work for them, or I could be on Wall Street moving around billion-dollar chunks of money.

But instead I was here, cold and anxious and very soon I'd have to drive the wet bike in front of one of these waves, dragging a beautiful redhead behind me on the end of a towline, and if -- when--she fell I'd have to go get her. Or die trying. That was the part I didn't like, the "die trying."

My name is T. R. Macdonald and believe it or not this was the good part. People hadn't started stuffing me in the trunks of cars or shooting at me. Yet.

Sailor Home From Sea

From the journals of T. R. Macdonald:

Westwood, CA. A UCLA Teaching Assistant is killed in a hit-and-run accident. But it's not an accident. It's murder.

Chicago, IL. A therapist at a prominent mental health clinic kills his girlfriend and then turns the gun on himself.

O'Hare International Airport Mary Shaw, aka Kandi, and the love of my life, is fleeing the scene of the murder-suicide when she is hacked. Her electronic life is destroyed and she is trapped with no ticket, no boarding pass, no cell phone, and no credit cards.

Huntington Beach, Surf City USA An artist named Mike Macdonald receives death threats. Mike's my father. Mike and Kandi need my help. The problem is, they don't want it. In fact, they don't want anything to do with me.

I'm down, but the surf's up.